THE GREAT CAT CONSPIRACY

Katie Davies

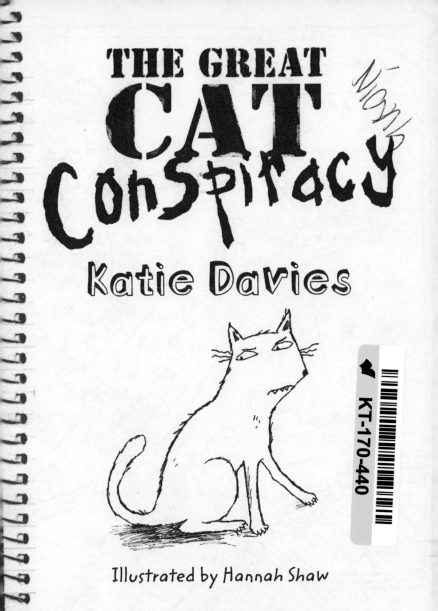

Illustrated by Hannah Shaw

SIMON AND SCHUSTER

For Harry, of course

Thanks to Alan, and Mum and Dad
and Venetia at Simon and Schuster.

First published in Great Britain in 2011 by Simon and Schuster UK Ltd,
a CBS company.

Text copyright © 2011 Katie Davies
Cover and interior illustrations copyright © 2011 Hannah Shaw
The story, *The Cat That Walked by Himself*,
is taken from Rudyard Kipling's *Just So Stories*, published 1902

Simon & Schuster UK Ltd
1st Floor, 222 Gray's Inn Road, London WC1X 8HB

A CIP catalogue record for this book is available from the British Library.

978-1-84738-596-3
1 3 5 7 9 10 8 6 4 2

Printed and bound in the UK by CPI Cox & Wyman, Reading RG1 8EX

www.simonandschuster.co.uk
www.katiedaviesbooks.com

🐾 CHAPTER 1 🐾
Cat Conspiracy

This is a story about Tom, and the Cat Lady, and everything that happened when the New Cat vanished. After it went missing, Mum said that me and Tom had to stop talking about the New Cat, and telling everyone how it had been kidnapped by the Cat Lady, and all that. She said, '*Anna*,' (that's my name) 'you can't go around accusing old ladies, and bandying words like "conspiracy" about, which you don't even understand.' But, like I told Tom, I *did* understand what a conspiracy was. Because me and my friend Suzanne looked it up in my dictionary, when we first heard there was one, off Graham Roberts at Sunday School.

1

And this is what it said:

conspiracy [kun-spir-uh-see] ✦ *noun*
an evil, unlawful, treacherous, or
surreptitious plan formulated in secret; plot

And what the dictionary said was probably
right. Because ours wasn't the only cat that had
vanished. Emma Hendry, in Mrs Peters' class,
couldn't find her cat, either. And nor could
Joe-down-the-road's babysitter, Brian. And
Graham Roberts said he had *seen* the Cat Lady
kidnapping cats, and taking them into her house,
himself. And he said, 'with my *very own eyes,*'
and swore it was true on Mrs Constantine's *life.*
Mrs Constantine is in charge at Sunday School.

She is the Vicar's wife.

Suzanne said that Graham swearing on Mrs Constantine might not count, because Graham sometimes lies. And you're only supposed to swear on the life of someone you *like*. And Graham didn't even have Mrs Constantine going to heaven when he did his big collage called, 'IT'S *JUDGEMENT* DAY!' Because he made her out of an egg box and she was too big to fit.

Anyway, like I told Mum, me and Tom did know *some* things about the Cat Lady, and where the New Cat was, and what had happened to it, and so did Suzanne. Because we were the ones who had sent out the Search Party. *And* we were the ones who were actually *in* it. And the whole *point* of a Search Party is to find things out.

It was Tom who first noticed that the New Cat had vanished. Tom is my brother. He's five. He's four years younger than I am. I'm nine. I've got another brother and a sister too, called Andy and Joanne, but they're not in this story because they're older than me and Tom and they don't really care about cats or conspiracies or anything like that.

If it wasn't for Tom, no one might even have minded that the New Cat had gone anywhere.

Because, before we couldn't find it, Tom was the only one in our house who cared about the New Cat, and what it got up to.

Mum said that *she* cared about what the New Cat got up to as well because, she said, '*I'm* the one who has to clean up after it all the time.'

But that isn't really the same kind of caring.

Most cats don't need to be cleaned up after. That's why Mum said we could get a new one, after our *Old* Cat died, and why we weren't allowed a dog, like me and Tom wanted. The New Cat isn't like most cats, though. The New Cat makes more mess than anyone's dog does. It makes more mess even than Tom. And it's not easy-to-clean-up-mess, either. Not like jigsaws, and sticklebricks, and Spiderman pants and all that. The mess that the New Cat makes is normally *dead*. Because, whenever it leaves the house, the New Cat *hunts*. And, after it's been hunting, it brings the things it has hunted inside, and puts them in places for people to find. Sometimes the things it brings in are still a bit alive. Like the hedgehog curled up in a ball, which it rolled in through the front door.

And the greenfinch with one wing, which was flapping behind the fridge. And the frog in the log basket, which me and Suzanne were going to bury, until we got it in the garden, and it hopped out of its box.

Most of the time, though, the things that the New Cat brings in are *definitely* dead. And sometimes they're so dead it's hard to tell what they *would* have been when they were *alive*. And that's when you only find a few feathers, or a bunch of bones, or a pile of slimy insides.

🐾 CHAPTER 2 🐾
The Petition

Suzanne lives next door. Her bedroom is right next to mine. If there wasn't a wall between our houses, our family and Suzanne's would live in one big house together, instead of two small houses apart, which would be a lot better. Because then me and Suzanne wouldn't have to ring on each other's doorbells, or bang on the wall, or shout through the letterbox every time we needed to talk. We could talk all the time, whenever we wanted, while we're supposed to be doing other things, like brushing our teeth, or remembering our spellings, or staying in our rooms until we've thought about what we've done.

I asked Mum if we could knock down the wall between our house and Suzanne's house.

Mum laughed, even though it wasn't funny, and said, 'You and Suzanne practically live together already.' Which isn't true because we only have our tea together on Tuesdays and Thursdays. And we aren't allowed to stay round each other's houses on school nights. And we don't go swimming together because Suzanne's got grommets.

This is what it says about 'grommets' in my dictionary:

grommet [grom-it] ✦ *noun*
a tube-shaped device used for the treatment of persistent middle ear infections where thick glue-like fluid builds up behind the ear drum

So me and Suzanne decided to do a Petition to see if we could get the wall knocked down that way, because, like Suzanne said, 'when you do a Petition, people can see you're serious.'

So we went in the shed, in the back lane, which only me and Suzanne are allowed into (except for Tom if he wants, when he remembers the password), and Suzanne wrote 'Purtishun' at the top of a piece of paper. And then she stopped because she said before she *wrote* the Purtishun, she just wanted to check exactly what one *was*. So we looked it up in the dictionary (which took a long time because Suzanne wasn't exactly sure how to spell it, either). This is what it said in my dictionary:

petition [puh-tish-un] ✦ *noun*
a formal request addressed to a person or persons in power, soliciting some favour, right, mercy or other benefit

And this is what it said in Suzanne's:

petition [puh-tish-un] ✦ *noun*
a document signed by a large number of people
demanding some action from the authorities

And, after that, we knew *exactly* what a petition
was. And Suzanne said we could probably write
one by ourselves but, just in case we might
miss something out, we should go and see
Mrs Rotherham up the road. Mrs Rotherham is
really old. Her house smells a bit strange, of old
things and mothballs, like Nanna's house used
to. But she's good at playing cards, and getting
everyone ice cream, and showing you how to do
things when you aren't exactly sure.

Mrs Rotherham said, 'A Petition? Sounds serious. You'd better come in.'

So we did. And we told her all about the wall, and how we thought it would be better if it wasn't there, because we couldn't talk to each other through it anymore, not since Suzanne's Dad took Suzanne's walkie-talkie off her, in the middle of the night, and rang on our doorbell in his dressing gown, and made Mum get me out of bed, and said, **'HAND THE DAMN THING OVER! IF I HEAR, "ANNA TO SUZANNE... ANNA TO SUZANNE" ONE MORE TIME, I'LL GO OUT OF MY MIND!'**

Mrs Rotherham listened and said, '*Well,*' and, 'I *see,*' and, 'Oh *dear*, oh dear, oh dear.' And she said she thought a Petition was *just* what was called for. And that she would start us off, and me and Suzanne could finish.

This is what our Petition said:

We **the undersigned** (which Mrs Rotherham said means 'we the people who have signed this underneath') **are in agreement that the wall between the Morris' house** (which is mine) **and the Barrys' house** (which is Suzanne's) **should be torn down in the name of peace and unity** and because it gets in the way and stops you being able to talk when you really need to, like in the middle of the night, when you aren't allowed out, and you haven't got walkie-talkies anymore, and you've thought of something important, which can't wait until the morning in case you forget it.

The people we got to sign it were…

A Morris (me)
S Barry (Suzanne)
K Rotherham (Mrs Rotherham)
C B (Carl Barry, Suzanne's brother)

Suzanne's Mum said Carl's signature didn't count because he's only a baby, and he can't write, and Suzanne must have held his hand. Which Suzanne admitted afterwards that she did, but only a bit.

We didn't exactly get a *large* number of people to sign the Petition, like Suzanne's dictionary said we should. Because getting people to put their names on was harder than we thought. Dad wouldn't sign it, and nor would Andy, or Joanne.

Even Tom wouldn't put his name on. And you can normally get Tom to do anything, as long as you give him a biscuit.

I showed Tom the Petition, and the biscuit, and he looked at it for ages. And then he said, 'What does it say?' Because he's only five and he can't really read yet, except for 'the', and 'cat', and his name. So I read the Petition out loud, and Tom asked, 'What does it mean?' So I told him how it was a serious thing, which people were putting their names on, to say they wanted the wall knocked down.

'What wall?'

'*This* one.'

'Why?'

'Because,' I said, 'if the wall isn't there, our family and Suzanne's will all live in one *big* house, which would be a lot better.'

Tom said, 'Where will Suzanne's Dad live?'

Suzanne told Tom her Dad would live in the house as well.

But Tom said he didn't want to live with Suzanne's Dad because 'he shouts too much.' Which is true. We hear him all the time through the wall, when he's **'COUNTING TO *THREE*'** and when he's **'NOT GOING TO SAY IT *AGAIN*'** and when he's **'LOSING THE WILL TO *LIVE!*'**

Suzanne said she didn't think her Dad would shout at anyone on *our* side of the house, because he will only be in charge of the people on *her* side.

But Tom wasn't sure. And he said he would rather keep the wall where it was. Because some of it was in his bedroom, and it had his bookshelf on, and his Batman stickers, and the bit he had coloured in black with a crayon. And he went and asked Dad for a biscuit instead.

I didn't say anything to Suzanne, but Tom was probably right about living with her Dad. And how he would be in charge.

Like he was the time our family and Suzanne's family went on a walk, which no one wanted to go on. He was definitely in charge of everyone then. Because he had a map, and a compass, and a stick that turned into a seat, which we weren't allowed to touch. And he told us what everything was, and how long it had been there. Like the bridge, and the battlements, and the boulders.

And there wasn't enough time to stop and

play Pooh Sticks. And he walked in front and said, **'ONLY NINE MORE MILES'** and **'WE WON'T BE BEATEN BY A BIT OF RAIN'** and *'RUN FOR COVER, FOR CRYING OUT LOUD!'*

And he made Tom leave all his best things behind, which he had been collecting on the way, like a brick, and a sheet of blue plastic, and a carrier-bag of gravel. Because he said Tom was slowing us down.

And after that Tom refused to walk at all, and he lay face down on the wet ground, and had what Nanna used to call the Screaming Habdabs. And Dad had to carry him the whole way home.

Anyway, it probably wouldn't have made any difference *how* many people me and Suzanne had got to sign the Petition. Because, when I showed it to Mum, she said, 'Don't be ridiculous, Anna. The wall is not coming down. This is a dictatorship, not a democracy. Get those aubergines eaten.'

This is what it says a dictatorship is in my dictionary:

Dictatorship [dik-tey-ter-ship] ✦ *noun*
a form of government in which absolute power is exercised by a dictator with imperious, overbearing control

And this is what it says a 'democracy' is:

Democracy [de-mok-ruh-see] ✦ *noun*
a form of government in which the supreme
power is vested in the people and exercised
by them or by their elected agents

I hate aubergines. Especially the ones off
Suzanne's Dad's allotment. Anyway, I stopped
wanting to get the wall down so much after that
because, for one thing, I thought Tom might be
right about living with Suzanne's Dad, and for
another thing, I found out that the wall had a *hole*
in it.

☙ CHAPTER 3 ☙
Three Blind Mice

The day I found out about the hole in the wall there was a strange smell in the house, like there is sometimes, when Mum stops what she's doing, and sniffs, and says, '*Ooh,* what on *earth* is *that?*'

And Dad says, 'What?'

And Mum says, 'I can *smell* something. Can't you?'

And Dad says, 'Nope.' And stares at the telly and tries not to talk about it.

And Mum goes sniffing round the house, on her hands and knees, until she finds out what it is. Sometimes it might be a mouldy potato in the bottom of the vegetable rack. Or dog poo that came in on someone's shoe, and got trodden into the carpet. But most of the time it's something that's dead somewhere, that the New Cat has dragged in from outside.

Mum followed the smell into the hall, until she came to the cupboard under the stairs, where the washing basket is, and the ironing pile, and all Dad's things, at the back, that aren't really allowed to be there, like the bag of worn-out footballs, and the broken tennis rackets, and the pile of newspapers he hasn't got round to reading yet. The cupboard under the stairs has got so much stuff in that, when you open the door, all the ironing falls out. And then you have to pick it all up, and shove it back in, and close the door quick, and put the catch down to keep it in. The cupboard under the stairs didn't *used* to have as much ironing in as it does now. Because, before Nanna died, whenever she came round, she always said, 'My programme's on in a bit. Get me set up, Duck, and I'll attack your ironing pile.'

And then Mum got the ironing board out. And put it up in front of the telly. And Nanna ironed everything, even things that Mum said were daft, like dishcloths, and hankies, and Tom's tiny pants. Because no one can iron as fast as Nanna could, or as neatly. And at the end of 'Coronation Street', Nanna stopped ironing and sat down. And Mum brought her half a cup of tea, in a china cup (because Nanna didn't like mugs and she said if she had more than half a cup she would be up and down to the toilet all night).

Anyway, this time, Mum was sniffing around. And when she came to the cupboard under the stairs, she stopped. And she opened the door. And all the ironing fell out. And she sniffed again, and said, 'Oh no, it's coming from in *here*.'

She sniffed through the ironing. And then she got the dirty washing basket out, and sniffed through that. (I wouldn't sniff the things in the

24

washing basket because it's full
of Andy's old football socks, and
Joanne's gymnastics leotards, and
Dad's dirty pants, but Mum doesn't
mind because she's a mum and that's what
they do.)

And, after that, Mum started pulling Dad's
things out of the cupboard as well, so she could
get right inside. And she piled them all up in
the hall. There was the alarm clock that doesn't
go off, and the toaster that doesn't pop, and the
kettle that me and Tom blew up by mistake.

Mum said, 'No wonder there's not enough
room for the ironing. It's like the electrical after-
life in here.' And she pulled out some more stuff. A
stool with one leg, and a bucket with a hole in the
bottom, and half a broom handle without a head.

Me and Tom sat on the stairs and watched. And Mum said, 'I thought I threw those out *years* ago.' And, 'Why on *earth* are we keeping *these*?' And, '*That's* as much use as a chocolate teapot.'

After a while, there was so much stuff in the hall that you could hardly see the carpet. When Mum got to the very bottom of the cupboard, she found a black bin bag. And she sniffed inside. And then she put her hand over her mouth, and made a sound like she was about to be sick, which went, 'Eur-*ugh*-eka!'

And she put a pair of rubber gloves on, and laid some newspaper on the floor. And she reached inside the bin bag, and started pulling things out, one at a time.

The bag was full of Dad's clothes from the olden days, like we've seen in photos, from before he was even bald. There was a flowery shirt with a flappy collar, and some purple velvet flares, like Willy Wonka wears, and some massive pants, with brown-and-orange stripes and a flap at the front, called Y-fronts.

Tom wanted to pull something out of the bag himself, because he said, 'It's a *lucky dip.*'

But Mum said, 'No! There's nothing lucky about it. Stand *back*, Tom, it stinks!'

And she reached in again, and felt around, and she pulled something out, and held it up in the air, by its tail, and she said *'Ah ha, a mouse!'* And she laid it on the newspaper. And then she tipped the bin bag upside down. And two more things fell out. And they were mice as well. Mum laid them on the newspaper, next to the first one.

Tom asked, 'Are they dead?'

'Dead?' Mum said, 'They're practically decomposed!' And then she shouted, *'PETE!'* (which is our Dad's name). Dad put the telly on pause and came into the hall. Mum pointed to the newspaper, with the mice on it, in a line.

And she said, 'What do you call this?'

Dad said, 'Urm… Three Blind Mice?' And he got The Hysterics (which is what you get when you start laughing and then you can't stop). And I got The Hysterics a bit as well. But Tom didn't, because he said he didn't think three blind mice were very funny, especially not when they were dead as well.

And neither did Mum, because she said, 'It's a mass grave, Pete, for goodness sake! The New Cat is disposing of its bodies in your bin bag.'

And she told Dad to start sorting all his stuff out, under the stairs, like she had been asking him to 'for ten years!' Because she said it was a breeding ground for bacteria, and a serious health hazard, and she had seen something on telly that said you shouldn't have anything in your house that isn't beautiful or useful.

And Dad said, 'Well, we'd better get rid of Anna in that case.' And he got The Hysterics again. But only a bit. Because nobody else did.

Mum said, 'I mean it. Two piles: one for the tip, and the other for the charity shop. I'm going to see Pam. I want it gone when I get back.'

Pam is Joe-down-the-road's Mum. She lives with Joe and Joe's New Rabbit at number 1.

And Tom went as well. Tom loves it at Pam's house, even on the weekends when Joe's at his Dad's and it's just Mum and Pam, drinking tea and talking about boring things. Like work, and washing, and Joe's Mum's New Boyfriend. Tom sits on Pam's knee and stays quiet, and eats all the biscuits.

I didn't want to go to Pam's. And sorting things

into piles and throwing them out isn't the kind of thing Dad is very good at, so I said I would stay and help. Because putting things in the bin is one of Dad's worst things. That's why he eats all the leftovers off mine and Tom's plates, which is good when it's aubergines, and Mum hasn't noticed, or the black bit in our bananas, or the skin off our fish. Dad eats the bits that no one wants, even when he's already full up himself. And then he says, 'Ugh, I've *eaten* too much' and has to go and lie down, in the dark, on the sofa, because he's too sick to help with the dishes.

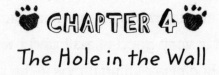

CHAPTER 4
The Hole in the Wall

Dad looked at all the things in the hall. And he started putting them into two piles. And, after a while, he said that instead of *two* piles, he would do *three*: one for the charity shop, one for the tip, and one for things that might come in useful. And he said we wouldn't need to tell Mum about the *third* pile because we could put it all up in the loft. In secret.

So I held each thing up, and said what it was. Like, 'a clock with no hands', and 'an umbrella with a hole in', and 'a shoe with no sole.' And Dad said which pile it should go in.

'Tip. No, Charity Shop. No, keep. Just *in case*.'

When we had finished, there was a small pile for the charity shop. And a small pile for the tip. And a BIG pile of 'useful' things to keep. And Dad said we had to hurry up and get the 'useful' pile up into the loft before Mum came back.

So he got the stepladder from the shed, and took it up to my room, where the hatch for the loft is. And he climbed up and opened it. And some dust, and dirt, and dead flies fell out on his head.

And I went downstairs and got as many things as I could carry from the 'useful' pile in the hall, and brought them back up, and passed them to Dad on the ladder. And I ran up and down doing that, as fast as I could. Because Dad said if we got it all done before Mum came back he would let me go up the ladder, into the loft, myself.

Without getting off the ladder, Dad balanced all the things on top of each other, close to the loft hatch. And when he was finished, he let me go up.

Dad handed me his torch. I had never been in the loft before. It was dark, and dusty, and Dad said there were bats. And he said you have to be careful to walk on the beams. Otherwise you can come straight through the ceiling.

'Quick, Anna, before Mum comes. And don't knock anything. If that lot falls through, my life won't be worth living.'

Careful not to knock Dad's pile of things, and holding on to the beams above me, I stepped from beam to beam towards a wall I could see across the other side. On my left the roof got lower and lower, and

34

on my right higher and higher. I reached the far wall, and ran my hand along. My hand went through a hole where some bricks were missing, and I grazed my arm.

'Hurry up,' Dad called out, 'don't go too far back.'

I shone my torch through the hole. I could see beams and boxes, just like in our loft. Only these boxes were all in rows, and they were on top of boards that had been put down.

'Alright, come back now, Anna.'

I stuck my head right through the hole, and squinted to see. Some of the boxes had writing on them. There were 'Christmas Decorations', and 'Camping

Equipment', and one of the boxes said 'Suzanne's old toys', in Suzanne's handwriting. The hole went straight into *Suzanne's loft.*

'Anna!' said Dad, 'If you don't come back now I'm closing the hatch.'

I went back the way I had come and, careful not to touch Dad's pile of useful things, I followed him back down the ladder.

'What were you doing?' Dad said.

'Urm, I saw a bat,' I said. And I slid down the ladder, and ran downstairs.

'Oi, I thought we were going to the tip? Wash your hands before Mum gets back. *Anna*?'

But I didn't answer. And I didn't have time to

wash my hands. And I hadn't seen a bat. I needed to see Suzanne to tell her about the hatch, and the loft, and the wall, and the hole.

I ran round to her house. And I rang on the Barrys' doorbell three times. Me and Suzanne always do three rings if it's something important.

And then I ran away again because it was a Saturday, which meant Suzanne's Dad would be home, and he doesn't like people ringing the doorbell more than once. He sticks his head out the window and says, **'YES? IS THERE A FIRE? I HEARD IT THE *FIRST TIME*, FOR CRYING OUT LOUD!'**

I waited in the shed until Suzanne came round. And I told her all about the hatch, and the loft, and the wall, and the hole.

'We need to do a plan,' Suzanne said. So we did. This is what the plan looked like when it was finished:

Since then, whenever me and Suzanne really need to talk, like in the middle of the night, when we aren't allowed out, and we've thought of something important, which can't wait until the morning, in case we forget it, I knock on Suzanne's wall three times and, if the coast is clear, Suzanne knocks back three times on mine. And then I climb up on my chest of drawers, and Suzanne climbs up on her wardrobe, and we reach up to the ceiling, and push the hatches back. And pull ourselves up on our arms, and scramble up inside. And we turn on our torches, and hold them in-between our teeth, because we need both hands to hold onto the roof, to balance from beam to beam, so we don't fall through the ceiling. And then we feel along the wall, and we meet at the hole. And we stay up there and talk about things, like the beams, and the bats, and whether there are holes in all the walls, in all the lofts, the whole way down the road. And how, if there are, you could climb through each one, and come out at the house at the bottom, which is Joe-down-the-road's.

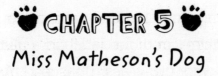

CHAPTER 5

Miss Matheson's Dog

Before the New Cat vanished, when it wasn't busy hunting, and killing things, and hiding their bodies round the house, it used to follow Tom around and watch what he was doing. Most of the things Tom does aren't that good for watching, like walking in a straight line with his eyes closed, or collecting gravel, or helping Mr Tucker pick up litter. But the New Cat didn't mind. It just waited nearby, with one eye open, watching Tom, and washing its whiskers.

Mr Tucker lives on the other side of the road, in the house opposite. When he was young, Mr Tucker was important in the War, flying planes, and fighting enemies, and getting shot at and all that. He's got lots of medals, and a pair of flying goggles with the glass smashed, and an old parachute to prove it. Mr Tucker doesn't fight enemies anymore. He's too old. Unless they've been throwing their beer cans into Mrs Tucker's chrysanthemums.

Mr Tucker was there when the New Cat *saved* Tom, the time he got attacked by Miss Matheson's dog. Mr Tucker was going up and down the road, picking up litter, like he always does, and Tom was with him, holding the bin bag for Mr Tucker to drop the litter into. And Mr Tucker was halfway inside a rose bush, trying to reach a packet of pickled onion Monster Munch. And Miss Matheson's dog got out. And it went running at Tom, barking, and baring its teeth. And Tom

42

panicked, and dropped the bin bag, and all the litter spilled out, and he ran off down the road. And Mr Tucker tried to untangle himself in the bush.

And Miss Matheson's dog chased Tom right down to the bottom of the road, and got him up against Joe-down-the-road's hedge. And, even though Miss Matheson's dog is only the same size as a guinea pig, Tom couldn't get away. Because, for one thing, Tom is only five, and he was born in August, and he's the smallest in his class, and that made Miss Matheson's dog seem much bigger. And, for another thing, Miss Matheson's dog isn't the kind of dog that people say, 'Oh, its bark is worse than its bite' about. It's the opposite kind of dog to that. Because its bark is only a yap. But, like the Milkman said, 'Its bite takes you by surprise.' And that's why he leaves Miss Matheson's milk on her wall, instead of taking it up to her doorstep.

GRR!

Anyway, Miss Matheson's dog was jumping up, and baring its teeth, and snapping between Tom's legs. And Mr Tucker was running down the road, to rescue Tom, when the New Cat came flying over the top of the hedge, hissing, with its ears flat, and its eyes wide, and its fur big. And it swiped Miss Matheson's dog right between the eyes. And Miss Matheson's dog yelped, and put its head between its paws. And the New Cat held it down on the ground with its claws. And then Miss Matheson came running down the road, in her slippers, with her coal shovel in her hand, and she whacked the New Cat on the head until it let her dog go. And she picked her dog up, and put it under her arm, and kissed it, and said, 'What are you doing to my *poor* little Misty?' and took it home.

If Miss Matheson hadn't come out, the New Cat would probably have dragged her dog in dead through the cat flap, like it does with everything else.

Anyway, after that, Mum

called, *'Anna…'*, the way she always does. And she came down the road. And she found me and Tom, and Mr Tucker (who had leaves and twigs and things stuck in his hair, and a tear in his shirt, and he'd left his blazer behind in the bush) and she said, 'Hello' to Mr Tucker, and Mr Tucker said, 'Hallo' back to Mum.

And then she said, 'What have you two been doing to Miss Matheson's dog?'

I said, 'Nothing.'

And Mum said how it didn't sound like *nothing* to her. Because, she said, 'Miss Matheson phoned. And she's *very* upset.'

And Miss Matheson had told Mum that me and Tom had been tormenting her dog, and setting the New Cat on it.

Mr Tucker said, 'Unreliable intell, Mrs Morris. Duff gen. Here's how it went. Dog comes flying out, full pelt, no provocation. Drives Basher downhill 'til his port engine packs up. Damned thing's got him frozen on the stick, up against the hedge here, going for his goolies, pardon my French. New Cat comes at it, low over the old hedge, and downs bandit with a single burst, bang on target. Then Miss M's out. Ten of the best to the New Cat's head. Tears a strip off the sprogs. Your mob not at fault. Wonder old Tommy here hasn't got the twitch.'

And then I told Mum what had happened as well. Because sometimes it's hard to understand what Mr Tucker means, with him being from the War. And Tom said how Miss Matheson's dog had tried to *kill* him,

47

and that the New Cat had *saved his life.*

Mum said, 'I think Miss Matheson's dog might be a bit small to kill you, Tom.'

Tom said, 'It's small, but it's nasty.'

And Mr Tucker said, 'I should say it is. Smallness inversely proportionate to its viciousness, Mrs Morris.' And he said the New Cat made a great Rear Gunner.

And Tom said, 'It's a *Guard* Cat.'

And Mr Tucker said, 'A Guard Cat, Basher, exactly that.'

And Tom stuck his chest out. And he gave Mr Tucker the salute. And Mr Tucker gave him the salute back.

I wasn't sure if the New Cat was *that* good a Guard Cat. Because, like I told Tom, it attacks things inside the house as well. Like *us*. And our *feet.* And a Guard Cat shouldn't do that, because we are the ones it's meant to guard. The New Cat even attacks Tom, if he hasn't got socks on.

Tom says the New Cat doesn't know that feet belong to *people.* Because, whenever it's wet outside, the New Cat stops hunting animals, and comes inside and hunts *us* instead. Sometimes it stands still, *just* inside a door, flat against the wall, and when the door opens, the New Cat flies out from behind it, and throws itself on your feet, and locks on with its claws, and sinks in its teeth. Other times, the New Cat goes part way up the stairs, and lies flat, pressing itself against a step, so you can't see it from the top, and when you step down onto the stair it's on, it shoots its paws out and gets you with its claws, and clings on to your ankle.

And sometimes the New Cat gets inside the beds, under the covers, right down at the bottom, and waits until you get in to go to sleep. And when you slide your feet down, it pounces, and gets its teeth in, and digs its claws into your toes, trapped under the covers.

And that's why everyone in our house has got scratches, and scabs, and scars on their feet.

And they're always running round in circles screaming, '*Help*, the *New Cat*!' and kicking their legs, to try to shake it off.

And that's why, when the New Cat first went missing, no one, apart from Tom, really cared very much.

☙ CHAPTER 6 ☙
The Vicar's Koi Carp

The night before it went missing, the New Cat caught a fish in the Vicarage pond. Not a small fish like Joe-down-the-road once won at the school summer fete. Or a middle-sized fish like Mum gets on Friday from the chip shop. This was a Really Big Fish. It was the biggest thing the New Cat had ever brought in. And it must have taken ages to catch it, and kill it, and drag it down the road, and get it in through the cat flap.

In the morning there were bits of fish all over the house. There was a tail on the kitchen table, and scales all up the stairs, and a backbone on the bathmat and, on Tom's pillow, when he woke up, was a big fish head with its eyes wide open.

I wouldn't like it if the New Cat put a fish head in *my* bed, but Tom didn't mind. He shouted out, 'Hey, Anna, come and see *this*.'

So I went into Tom's room. And he sat up in bed. And he pointed at his pillow.

'It's a fish head,' I said.

Tom said, 'Do you think it's a present from the New Cat?'

And I said I thought it probably was. Because I didn't think anyone else would give a present like that.

'The New Cat likes me *best*,' Tom said. And he got out of bed, and he picked up the fish head, and he took it into Mum's room, where she was still asleep, and said, '*Look!*' And he held it near Mum's face.

Mum opened her eyes, and said, '*What the…? Tom,* it's a *fish head*!'

And Tom said, 'Yes.'

'Where did you *get* it?'

'In my bed.'

'Give me *strength,*' Mum said. And she looked at her clock, and then she shot out of bed, because she had overslept. And she grabbed the fish head off Tom, and ran downstairs, and she got the tail off the kitchen table, and put them both in the bin. And then she ran back up, and brushed her teeth, and picked the bones up off the bath mat, and hoovered the trail of scales all up the stairs.

And she said, 'I'm going to Church…'

Because it was Sunday. 'If anyone's interested? *Stinking* of *fish*.'

Mum didn't used to go to Church much because she only went sometimes to keep Nanna company. But, after Nanna died, when it was her funeral, Mrs Constantine asked Mum if she could put her name down on the handing out the hymn book rota. And Mum meant to say 'no', but she said 'yes', by mistake. And after that she had to go to Church all the time. Because the other people who hand out the hymn books were always going away on holiday, and getting glandular fever, and things like that.

When Mum goes to Church, me and Tom go to Sunday School, next door, and do painting, and putting on plays instead, and Tom eats all the biscuits.

Dad doesn't go to Church. He doesn't even believe in God. He says he believes in staying in bed.

After Church was over, and the Vicar had finished standing by the door, and shaking everyone's hands, and saying, 'Go in peace and serve the Lord,' he came back inside where Mum was putting the hymn books away, and I was waiting, and Tom was collecting up all the cushions for kneeling, and putting them in a big pile by the pulpit (which is the thing the Vicar stands on to speak). And the Vicar said, 'Hello,' and, 'Lovely day,' and 'Put the cushions back now, please.' And then he asked Tom what we had done in Sunday School.

Tom said how we had eaten biscuits.

55

And the Vicar said, 'Anything *else*?'

And Tom shook his head.

And the Vicar said, 'I'm sure you *did*. I know Mrs Constantine was going to do the story of the loaves and the fishes with you, and make a start on the frieze for the far wall.' Which she probably was, but Graham Roberts put the lock on when he went to the loo, which we're not supposed to do, because he forgot about it again, and he didn't see the big sign that says, 'DO NOT USE THIS LOCK. IT GETS STUCK!'

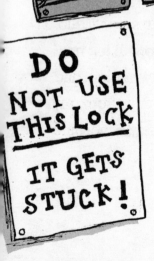

So Mrs Constantine had to go and get the caretaker, and this time he had to take the door off. And everyone watched. And after that there was only time to do the prayer, and have juice and biscuits.

Anyway, the Vicar asked Tom if he knew the story about Jesus and the five loaves, and the two fishes, and how he had fed the five thousand.

And Tom said he didn't.

And the Vicar said how it was from the Gospel according to St John, from Matthew, chapter 14, verses 13 to 21. And he asked Tom if he would like to hear it.

And Tom said, 'No thanks.'

The Vicar didn't look very pleased. And he breathed in deep, and he did a sigh. And then he did a sniff. And he said, 'Can anyone else *smell fish*?'

Mum stopped putting the hymn books away.

And the Vicar said, 'I've got fish on the brain. Several of mine have gone missing from my pond. There was another one gone this morning when I got up - my best Koi Carp.'

Mum didn't say anything. But Tom did. He said, 'Mum smells of fish.'

The Vicar said, 'I'm sure she doesn't.'

Tom said, 'She does, because the New Cat brought a big fish in through the cat flap and it killed it and put its bits all over the house. And Mum had to clean it up. Its head was on my pillow.'

And the Vicar said, 'Oh? What did this fish *look* like?'

And Tom said, 'Like *this.*'

And he held his eyes wide apart and rolled them around and stuck his tongue out.

And the Vicar said, 'What colour was it?'

And Tom told the Vicar how it was hard to tell what colour it was because it was in lots of different bits because its scales were all up the stairs, and its tail was on the table, and its bones were on the bathmat. And some of it was missing, but its head, which was in his bed, was white and orange with black spots.

And the Vicar said, 'That's my best *Koi Carp*! I bought him for breeding…'

And Tom said, 'He's in the bin.' And then he said, 'Are there any more biscuits?'

And the Vicar said, '*No.* There *aren't.*' And his neck went all red.

And Mum said, 'I am so sorry about your Koi Carp. Can we buy you a replacement?'

The Vicar said, 'If you insist.'

Which Mum hadn't. Because she only said it once. And if you insist about something you say it lots of times. Over and over again. Until the other person gives in. But Mum got her purse out of her handbag and said, 'How much is it?'

The Vicar said, 'Two hundred and twenty pounds.'

Mum looked surprised. And then she looked in her purse.

The Vicar said, 'I can take a cheque.'

And Mum said, 'Oh… right... yes.'

And she got her cheque-book out, and wrote 'two hundred and twenty pounds' on one. And she gave it to the Vicar. And he put it in his pocket.

👑 BANK-O   30-01-02

Mr R. Constantine

Two hundred and

twenty pounds ONLY—   £220=

"1020304" 302010: 636365208111

When we got home, Dad was still in bed. And me and Tom went in to bounce on it, and wake him up, and Mum came as well, and she told him about the Vicar's Koi Carp, the New Cat, and the cheque for two hundred and twenty pounds.

Dad said the Vicar would be lucky if there was two hundred and twenty pounds in their bank account. And then he said, 'That's *enough bouncing*.' And he got out of bed, and started going downstairs to make breakfast, saying things to himself, about the Vicar, and how he should spend less on his pond and more on the poor, like he's always on about.

The New Cat was halfway up the stairs, lying flat against a step, so Dad couldn't see it, and it probably hadn't had its breakfast either, because

61

when Dad put his foot down onto the stair it was on, the New Cat shot out its paws, and clung on with its claws, and sank in its teeth. And Dad screamed, 'Agh, the **NEW CAT!**' And he fell down the rest of the stairs, with the New Cat attached.

When he got to the bottom, he kicked the air until the New Cat came flying off, and hit the wall, and then, while it was still stunned, Dad grabbed the New Cat by the scruff of its neck, and put it out the back door. And slammed the door shut. And said, **'AND STAY OUT!'** And after that Dad put the lock down on the cat flap.

Tom asked Dad to take the lock off. Because he said it wasn't the New Cat's fault, really, about the Vicar's fish. Because cats are *supposed* to catch things. And they don't know how much they cost. And he told Dad how the New Cat didn't know that feet belonged to people. And how it didn't like it outside. Because it was raining. And that was why it kept running at the cat flap, and banging its head.

But Dad just said, 'Tough.' And put the bacon under the grill, and cracked the eggs into the frying pan, and turned the radio right up.

And the New Cat put its tail in the air, and walked away down the road.

And Tom watched it through the window.

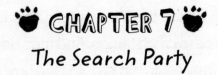

CHAPTER 7

The Search Party

The New Cat hadn't come back by the time we went to bed.

In the morning, which was Monday, when Tom woke up, he asked, 'Has the New Cat come back?'

And Mum said, 'No.'

And when Tom got home from school, he asked again, 'Is the New Cat back?'

And Mum said, 'Not yet.'

And on Tuesday, and Wednesday, and Thursday, and Friday, Tom asked again about the New Cat, and where it was, and whether it was coming back. And, when Saturday came,

Tom wouldn't sit with me and have his cereal, in his pyjamas, and watch cartoons, or go and meet Suzanne to make plans in the shed. He put his wellies on instead, and went down the road, on his own, and stood at the bottom, and looked up and down.

Mr Tucker was out picking up litter, and he saw Tom standing at the bottom of the road, and he gave him the salute and called down, 'Out early today, Old Chum. Getting a head start on collecting the gravel up, eh?'

Tom shook his head.

'Walking-in-a-straight-line-with-the-old-eyes-closed today, is it?'

Tom shook his head.

'How about plugging away with me at this

litter situation, then?'

Tom shook his head again.

So Mr Tucker went down the road, and he sat on the wall at the bottom, and Tom sat down too. And he said, 'Not *woman trouble*, is it, Old Chap?'

And Tom said it wasn't, and he told Mr Tucker all about what had happened with the New Cat, and the Vicar's fish, and how it had hunted Dad's feet. And how Dad had thrown it out. And locked the cat flap. And how he didn't think it was coming back.

Mr Tucker said, 'Old Rear Gunner missing in action, eh? Black do all round, Basher. Can't have that. What about a recce, eh? Send out a search party, Tom, what do you say?' Tom wiped his nose on his sleeve. And Mr Tucker got his hankie out, and he held it to Tom's nose, and said, 'Give it a good blow.' And Tom did. And then he said, 'That's the ticket. Now, look tidy. Fling one up.'

And Tom stood up straight. And he gave Mr Tucker the salute. And Mr Tucker gave him the salute back. And he took Tom down into the village. And they asked everyone they passed if they had seen the New Cat. And no one had. And Mr Tucker told Tom he thought that the New Cat had probably gone on holiday, or something like that. And it was sure to come back. Because cats were always doing things like that. And he had heard of one cat that went to Spain on a ferry. On its own. By mistake. And it came back in the end. Because, he said, 'Thing with cats is, *top notch navigators.*'

After they had been round the village, and asked in all the shops, and bought a bag of sweets, and stopped halfway up the hill for a rest on the bench - while Mr Tucker had his puffer, and Tom wet his wellies in the horse trough - they walked back up into our road. Mrs Tucker came out, and Mr Tucker said, 'Hallo, Tom, look sharp, Squadron Leader.'

Mrs Tucker said, 'Hello Poppet' to Tom, and she said, '*Raymond!* Where have you been?'

And Mr Tucker said, 'Reconnaissance, Dickey. Tom's cat's gone AWOL.'

Mrs Tucker said, 'Oh dear, poor old Tom, I'm sorry to hear *that.*'

68

And then she said, 'Raymond, your breakfast is cold, and you're late to take your pills, and in case you've forgotten, your cousins are *still* here.'

Mr Tucker said, 'Roger that. T minus two minutes, Dickey.'

And he asked Tom, 'Where's the rest of your wing? Popsie and so on?' Popsie is what Mr Tucker calls me. Even though it's not my name. And I've told him I don't like it.

Tom told Mr Tucker I was in the shed, making plans with Suzanne.

'Old chairborne division, eh?' And he told Mrs Tucker to take Tom inside and give him a biscuit. 'Back in a jiffy.'

And he went round the side of our house, into the back lane. And he knocked on the shed door.

Me and Suzanne looked through the spy hole,

69

which is a knot of wood at the front of the shed that you can pop in and out.

Suzanne said, 'What's the password?'

'Press On Regardless.'

Which it wasn't. But we opened the door anyway because Mr Tucker had never knocked on the shed before so it was probably important. He came inside, and he looked at the wasp trap, and the worm box, and he tried to look at the plan that me and Suzanne were working on. Which we hadn't got very far with because we had only done the title, which was too long, and took up most of the piece of paper. It said:

Anna's And Suzanne's Plan To Find Out If There Are Holes In All The Walls In All The Lofts In All The Houses In The Road And, If There Are, Whether We Can Climb Through Them And Come Out In The House At The Bottom, Which is Joe-Down-The-Road's.

I rolled the plan up so Mr Tucker couldn't see it.

Mr Tucker said, 'Look here, I can see you bods are hard up against it with your bumph and all that, but this briefing comes down from Brass Hats, so look lively; simple enough op for your division, Popsie. As of eleven hundred hours, we want all personnel assisting Basher with this damned Cat Situation. Went AWOL on Sunday, of course, and so far it's still Missing In Action. Don't like to mention moral fibre, or the lack of, but it doesn't do to leave a chap's cat unaccounted for, so fingers out for you and Blondie on this one, eh Popsie, what do you say?'

I said, 'Okay.'

And Mr Tucker said, 'That's the ticket. Best

of British. Your group's got the green, Popsie, chocks away.'

And he gave the salute. And Suzanne gave him the salute back. But I didn't, because the last time I gave Mr Tucker the salute, which was ages ago, when I was about eight, Mr Tucker said I didn't do it right, and he made me do it again, about a million times, and he kept saying, 'more power on the up.' And also because I didn't really *want* to try to find the New Cat, because I wanted to do the plan for the loft and the holes, and climbing through all the houses in the road, and coming out at the bottom in Joe-down-the-road's.

Tom came to the shed with the biscuits from Mrs Tucker. And Mr Tucker said, 'Right-o. Relatives now, Basher. Black do all round.'

And he messed Tom's hair up. And then he went home.

When he was gone, Suzanne said how she didn't know why Mr Tucker called her 'Blondie' when her hair was brown. And she said, 'I don't know why he says that it's *your* division, and *your* group, either, because it's not like you're in charge.' Which is true. Because normally Suzanne is. Especially when it comes to investigations. Because Suzanne knows everything about stuff like that, because her Mum lets her watch all the police dramas on telly, and one of her uncles is a Special Constable, and she's got a book from the Brownie Jumble sale called, *Private Detective: A Practical Handbook.* Which she keeps under her bed. And she's read it a billion times.

Suzanne said, 'You didn't tell me the New Cat was missing.'

Which was true, because I forgot. And because I didn't really care about the New Cat. Not until Tom came into the shed, after Mr Tucker left, and his eyes were all red, and his t-shirt was wet, and he was chewing his coat sleeve like he sometimes does when he's upset.

And he said, 'Are you making a plan for finding the New Cat?'

And then I said, 'Yes.' And so did Suzanne.

And Tom stopped chewing his sleeve, and he sat down, and starting eating his biscuits.

And Suzanne put the plan for the loft and the holes behind the stepladders, under the shelf with the wasp trap on and the worm collection. And I got my dictionary and I looked up 'AWOL'.

Because that's what Mr Tucker said the New Cat was.

And this is what it said:

AWOL [A.W.O.L] ♦ *noun*
Absent With Out Leave (A.W.O.L) – normally used about a soldier or other military person who is absent from duty without permission, but without the intention of deserting

🐾 CHAPTER 8 🐾

What Might Have Happened to the New Cat

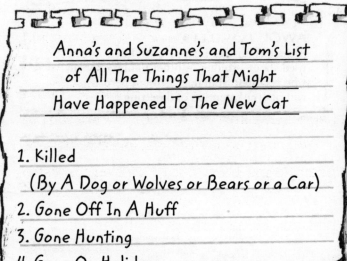

Anna's and Suzanne's and Tom's List
of All The Things That Might
Have Happened To The New Cat

1. Killed
   (By A Dog or Wolves or Bears or a Car)
2. Gone Off In A Huff
3. Gone Hunting
4. Gone On Holiday

The first thing on the list was 'Killed'. I didn't think a dog would be able to kill the New Cat because we had never met one that it was even scared of. And Tom agreed, because he said, 'In a fight with a dog, the New Cat would win. But,' he said, 'it might not win against wolves or bears. Especially if they were hungry, or in a big pack.'

· You don't really get packs of wolves or bears round here, but I put it on the list anyway because Tom's eyes were still pink and he had finished all his biscuits.

I said maybe the New Cat had been got by a car. Like happened to our *Old* Cat, in the back lane, when Miss Matheson ran it over.

But Suzanne said she didn't think Miss Matheson *had* run over the *New* Cat, because when she ran the Old Cat over, Suzanne found cat blood on Miss Matheson's car tyres. And there wasn't any blood on them this time, because Suzanne had checked. And anyway, like Tom said, we didn't *just* find cat blood when the Old Cat got run over. Because we also found the Old Cat, squashed flat, out the back, by Miss Matheson's gate. And no one had found the New Cat squashed flat anywhere.

So we crossed number 1, 'Killed (By A Dog or Wolves or Bears Or A Car)' off.

Number 2 on the list was 'Gone Off In A Huff'. Which was Suzanne's idea. Suzanne goes off in huffs, if you do something she doesn't like, and then you have to wait for ages, and try and find her, and say sorry, and all that. But the New Cat doesn't go in for huffs much, because it's not the sort of cat that wants people coming after it. You can't even touch it without gardening gloves on. And, anyway, the New Cat had been gone for nearly a week. And even Suzanne has never stayed in a huff *that* long. But Suzanne said that she would, if she had been thrown out, and it was raining, and she kept banging her head on the cat flap.

So we went up and down the road, looking for the New Cat, and we put bits of ham out, and banged on a saucer of milk with a spoon, and shouted, 'Puss, puss, puss, puss, puss.' Like Nanna sometimes did, before she died, to get the Old Cat to come in at night. But the New Cat didn't come.

So we crossed **'Huff'** off the list as well.

The next thing was **'Gone Hunting'**. Because, like Suzanne said, 'The New Cat is always off killing things. And maybe it has had to go further to find some, because it has already killed all the things in the garden, and there probably wasn't anything left alive, nearby.'

But Tom told Suzanne how the New Cat always brings the things it has hunted back, to hide them in the house. And how it doesn't go hunting when it's wet outside. Because that's when it stays in, and sleeps, and hunts feet in the house. And it had been raining all week. So we crossed **'Gone Hunting'** off too.

Tom said the New Cat might have **'Gone On Holiday'**, like Mr Tucker said. And he told us about the cat that went to Spain on the ferry by itself,

NEW CAT ↓ ← FERRY

80

by mistake, and found its way back. Suzanne said she didn't think cats went on holiday on their own, even if it wasn't on purpose, because she thought that was only the kind of thing that grown ups say to shut you up and stop you getting upset. So we went into the house and put 'cat, Spain, holiday, mistake' into the computer. And what Mr Tucker said was true. Because there was a picture of the cat, and it had got in the news. And it said:

Missing Moggie Found On Ferry

Stowaway Sandi was discovered by stunned ferry staff under a lorry on the *P&O Pride of Bilbao*, which had travelled all the way from Portsmouth. The ferry crew took the tom to a vet who was able to tell from an embedded microchip where he was from. Sandi had a luxurious return trip, fed on a special menu of fresh salmon, grilled chicken and milk in an en-suite cabin with a sea view.

But the New Cat didn't have an embedded microchip. It didn't even have a collar, so no one would know where to bring it back to. And, like Suzanne said, it could have got off the boat in Spain, or something like that. And we couldn't go there to look for it, because Suzanne isn't even allowed past the bottom bus stop because her Dad says it's **'OUT OF BOUNDS.'** And that meant all we could do was wait, to see if the New Cat came home. Which wasn't much of a plan. And that was all the things on our list.

So I said, 'Let's go and see Mrs Rotherham.' And Suzanne said that was a good idea, because of how Mrs Rotherham used to be in the police so she knows about these kinds of things. And Tom said it was a good idea too. Because Mrs Rotherham always has biscuits.

🐾 CHAPTER 9 🐾
The Suspect List

We told Mrs Rotherham all about what had happened with the New Cat and the Vicar's Koi Carp and how Dad had thrown it out and locked the Cat Flap, and how it still hadn't come back. And Mrs Rotherham went and made some tea, and Tom asked if she had any biscuits, and she brought out the tin, and she said, 'When I was in the police,' which was probably about a million years ago, 'the first thing we did when a person went missing was to fill out a *Missing Person Alert* form.' And she went inside her cupboard. And she found a form. And she brought it out. And she crossed 'Person' out, and put 'Pet' instead. And me and Tom and Suzanne sat by the fire and drank the tea and ate the biscuits and filled it in. And when it was finished the Missing Pet Alert Form looked like this: ⟶

Mrs Rotherham looked at the form and said she thought it was very good.

Suzanne asked, 'What did you do after that?'

'I'd ask myself, has this person gone somewhere of their own accord, or are we dealing with something altogether more untoward? Then I'd do some poking about the place. More often that not, if there's a suspect, it'll be someone very close to the person who's missing. A neighbour, maybe. A family member, more often than not. And then it's motive, of course, and whether or not the suspect had an opportunity,

Missing ~~Person~~ PET Alert

SURNAME: Cat

FORENAME: The New

DOB (Mrs Rotherham said this means Date of Birth): Unknown

PHYSICAL DESCRIPTION: small, angry animal with four legs and a tail

HEIGHT: About up to Tom's new bruise

BUILD: scrawny

HAIR, COLOUR AND STYLE: Grey, matted

EYE COLOUR: Green

CLOTHING: None (it used to have a flea collar but it chewed it off)

ANY DISTINGUISHING FEATURES: A tooth that hangs down over its mouth

KNOWN RISKS: Hunts most things, especially birds, mice, moles, voles, rats, rabbits, spiders, wasps, flies and feet

ADDITIONAL INFORMATION: Do not approach without gardening gloves

CONTACT DETAILS: Anna and Tom Morris, Number 5, Spoutwell Lane and are there any prior convictions?'

Suzanne wrote down everything that Mrs Rotherham said in the notepad.

'After that, it's a rather less interesting business. Putting up "Missing" posters, talking to passers-by, handing out fliers. Offer a reward.'

We finished our tea. And Tom ate the last biscuit. And Suzanne finished writing, and put the notepad in her pocket. And we said, 'thank you' to Mrs Rotherham. And went back down the road.

When we got back to the shed, Suzanne wrote on the top of a piece of paper, <u>People Who Might Have Taken The New Cat</u> and she underlined it.

I said I couldn't think of anyone who would take the New Cat. Because it wasn't the sort of cat that people would want. Because, before it went missing, *we* didn't even want it ourselves.

Tom said, 'Someone might take it to make a fur coat, like Cruella de Vil does in *101 Dalmatians*.'

But I didn't think *anyone* would wear the *New Cat's* coat. Even if it was washed, and had conditioner put on it, and got given a blow dry. Because the New Cat's coat isn't very nice, and it's got lots of bits missing from all the times it's been in fights.

Suzanne said, 'There might be another reason why someone would take it.'

And I said, 'Like what?'

And Suzanne said, '*Revenge.*' And then she wrote on the paper:

1. The Vicar, for killing his Koi Carp
2. Miss Matheson, for attacking her dog
3. Anna's Dad, for costing £220 to buy the Vicar a new fish

I thought Suzanne might be right about the Vicar and Miss Matheson, but I didn't think Dad really wanted revenge much, because all he ever wants is to watch football, and drink beer, and he probably couldn't be bothered to kidnap the New Cat.

But Suzanne looked in the notepad, at all the things Mrs Rotherham had said, and she read, *'More often than not it's a family member.'* And she wrote, Motive? Yes. Opportunity? Yes. And then she said, 'Has your Dad got any prior convictions?'

And I said, 'I don't know.'

And Suzanne wrote, Possible prior convictions. And she underlined Anna's Dad. And she put the notepad in her pocket, and she got the binoculars, and she said, 'Let's go to the Vicarage.'

And Tom asked us to wait while he went inside, and got his swimming goggles, even though, like Suzanne said, 'You won't really need them.'

And we went up the road.

🐾 CHAPTER 10 🐾
Poking About The Place

Suzanne looked through the Vicarage gate with the binoculars. And then I looked as well. And then Tom. But none of us could see the New Cat, especially not Tom because he had his goggles on, and the binoculars back to front. And then we opened the gate and went in because, like I told Suzanne, it was a Saturday, so the Vicar would be doing weddings.

We put the binoculars through the letterbox, and up to all the windows at the front of the house. And then me and Suzanne went round the back. And Tom stayed at the front, behind the hedge, to keep watch.

Me and Suzanne looked through the binoculars into all the windows at the back. And we couldn't see the New Cat there, either.

Suzanne said, 'The New Cat isn't the sort of animal that someone could take easily.' Which was true. 'Which means there was probably a fight. So if the Vicar took it, we should see signs of a struggle.'

So we went all round the Vicarage looking for some. But we didn't find any. And, after a while, Suzanne said, 'The New Cat isn't here.' So we went back round to the front.

When we got there, Tom wasn't standing behind the hedge, looking out. He was lying on the ground, with his face in the fishpond.

'Tom?!' I said. 'What are you doing?'

Tom lifted his head up. 'I'm looking for the

New Cat, in case the Vicar has drowned it.' And he put his face back in the water, and blew out, so bubbles came up, like he learnt at swimming club. And then his head came up again, and he said, 'It's not here.' And he wiped his goggles with his sleeve, and his tongue as well, because he said, 'I forgot to close my mouth,' and it had quite a lot of green slime on.

And then we went down the road, and round the back, to Miss Matheson's.

We got down on the tarmac in the back lane beside Miss Matheson's fence, and looked through the binoculars.

I said if she *had* taken the New Cat, I didn't think Miss Matheson would keep it in the garden. Because, for one thing, it would be too easy for it to escape. And, for another thing, someone might spot it. And, for an even other thing, it might attack Miss Matheson's dog.

And Tom said he didn't think Miss Matheson would keep the New Cat in her house either, because it would hunt her feet, and tear up her furniture, and it might attack her dog there as well.

And Suzanne said that she thought we were right, and if Miss Matheson was going to keep the New Cat anywhere, it would have to be in her garage, and it would probably be tied up.

So me and Suzanne and Tom climbed over the gate, and we crept over the gravel, and ran over to the garage, and I gave Suzanne a boost up, and she looked in through the garage window.

93

And then we swapped around.

Miss Matheson's garage was very neat. There were rakes and brooms and hoes all in a line. And plant pots in order of size. And one shelf for jars, and another for paint, and one for string and twine. But there wasn't any sign of the New Cat anywhere.

'It's not here,' I said.

I got down from the garage window. And we started walking back towards the gate. And when we were half way across we stopped, because we heard someone say, 'Ah hem.'

Miss Matheson was standing on the other side of the gate.

In the back lane. With her arms crossed. Watching us. And Mum was standing beside her.

Miss Matheson said, 'This is the kind of thing I'm talking about, Mrs Morris.' And she said how she wasn't the only one in the street who was upset with our family, and our pets. Because she had spoken to the Vicar, and he had told her about our cat, and what it had done to his Koi Carp. And she had seen us all in his garden, just now, meddling in his pond.

And Mum said, '*Anna*, is that true?'

And I said, 'No.'

And Mum said, 'Why has Tom got goggles on? And what's that green slime?'

And Mum took me and Tom and Suzanne inside.

And Miss Matheson called, 'If it happens once more, I shall call the *police*.'

Suzanne said that we could call the police on Miss Matheson, actually, because of her dog, and how it attacked Tom. Because she said, 'Miss Matheson's dog should wear a muzzle.' Which Suzanne knows all about from when her cousin went to court.

Mum said she was pretty sure Miss Matheson's dog wasn't covered by the Dangerous Dogs Act, because it was a Chihuahua, and they didn't have to have muzzles on. And then she said, 'And in any case, Suzanne, that's not the point.'

And Tom said, 'What does "the point" mean?'

And Mum said, 'It means you had no business going in her garden, and looking into her garage. Or the Vicar's. What were you doing?'

I didn't say anything and nor did Suzanne. Tom said, 'The Vicar and Miss Matheson have taken the New Cat, and drowned it and tied it up and things like that.'

And Mum said, 'No one has taken the New Cat, Tom.'

And she said me and Suzanne had to stop filling Tom's head with rubbish. Because it wasn't fair, and it wasn't funny.

And I said how it wasn't meant to be funny because, I said, 'It's very serious. And that's why me and Suzanne and Tom are trying to find it.'

Mum said, 'If someone's got the New Cat, it's more likely to have been *adopted* than *abducted*.'

I got my dictionary and looked 'adopted' up.
This is what it said:

adopt [ad-o-pt] ✦ *verb*
to choose or make one's own by selection;
to rear as one's own

And this is what it said about 'abducted':

abduct [ab-duck-t] ✦ *verb*
to carry off or lead away in secret or by force,
often using threats or violence; to kidnap

But whether the New Cat had been abducted
or adopted didn't make much difference, I didn't
think. Because you can't just go round adopting
pets that already belong to other people.

Because, I said, 'Imagine if someone just came and adopted me or Tom?'

Mum said, 'Ha. *Imagine!*'

And she told us to we had to play inside for a while.

And Suzanne got the notepad out and crossed the Vicar and Miss Matheson off the list because, like she said, we had done a search, and we hadn't seen the New Cat, and there weren't any signs of a struggle. And Miss Matheson would have had scratches on her hands if she had touched the New Cat. And she didn't, because Suzanne had checked. And that meant there was only one person left. And that was *Dad*.

'Let's interrogate him.' Suzanne said.

This is what my dictionary says interrogate means:

interrogate [in-ter-o-gate] ✦ *verb*
to ask someone a lot of questions for a long time in order to get information, sometimes using threats or violence

Suzanne said, 'We need to do a lie detector test.'

Because, she said, her book tells you all about how when people tell lies, their eyes look up, and off to the left, and they touch their mouths with their hand.

So she said, 'We'll ask him all about the New Cat, and what has happened to it. And the lie detector test will say if he's telling the truth.'

Dad was watching football with his hands over his eyes.

I told him how we were trying to find out what had happened to the New Cat.

Dad said, 'Uh huh.' Like he does when he isn't listening.

So I said how it was very important and we needed to ask him some questions.

And Dad said, 'Yup.'

And I said, 'Now.'

And Dad said, 'Yeah, yeah.' And then he said, 'At half time.'

And Suzanne said, 'Or we could go and tell your Mum about the loft, Anna, and how all the broken things from under the stairs are up there.'

And then Dad jumped up, out of his chair, and said, 'No, no, don't do that! I'll answer your questions.'

And Suzanne said, 'I thought so.' And she turned the telly off. And she told Dad to turn his chair around. And she closed the curtains. And she turned on the lamp, and she pointed it at Dad. And she walked around the room.

And she whispered to me to ask Dad a question I knew he would lie to, so I said, 'Do you

101

like going on long walks with Suzanne's Dad?'

And Dad said, 'Urm, yes, I do.' And he touched his mouth and his eyes went up to the left. And Suzanne said, 'That's a *lie!* Ask him again.'

So I said, 'I'm going to ask you again. Do you like going on walks with Suzanne's Dad?'

And Dad said, 'Urm, well, no, not that much.' And he didn't put his hand on his mouth, or move his eyes. So we knew that the lie detector test was working.

And after that Suzanne asked Dad lots of questions really fast, close to his face, like, 'Do you like the New Cat?' and, 'Are you glad it's gone?' and, 'Do you hope it never comes back?'

And Dad said, 'Urm, no, yes, I do, I'm sorry, Tom.'

And Suzanne said, 'And that's why you took it

and tied it up, or killed it, isn't it?'

And Dad said, 'What? Oh, yes, of course, that's *exactly* it.' But his hand touched his mouth, and his eyes went up, and to the left, which meant he was lying.

And then Tom went very close up to Dad, with the lamp, and he pointed it right in his face, and Dad said, '*Ah*, I'm *blind*.'

And Tom said, 'Have you kidnapped the New Cat, Dad?' And he looked right in his eyes.

And Dad said, 'No, Tom, of course not.' And it wasn't a lie because he looked straight back at Tom and his hand didn't touch his mouth.

So Suzanne said, 'No further questions.'

And she opened the curtains, and turned the lamp off, and put the telly back on, and Dad turned his chair around and started watching the

103

football again.

And me and Tom and Suzanne went back to
the shed and looked in the notepad for what Mrs
Rotherham said to do next.

☙ CHAPTER 11 ☙

Missing

The next thing after 'poking about to see if it's a neighbour or a family member' was to put up 'Missing' posters and hand out fliers, and offer a reward.

So Suzanne drew two pictures of the New Cat, one big one for the poster and a smaller one for the flier. And Tom started colouring them in.

And then Suzanne had to draw the big one again, because Tom put green stripes on the New Cat's body, and gave it red feet which, like Suzanne said, was nice, but wasn't exactly what the New Cat looked like.

And she told Tom to colour the New Cat in

grey, so people would know what cat it was. And when the pictures were finished, I put the words on.

This is what the poster looked like:

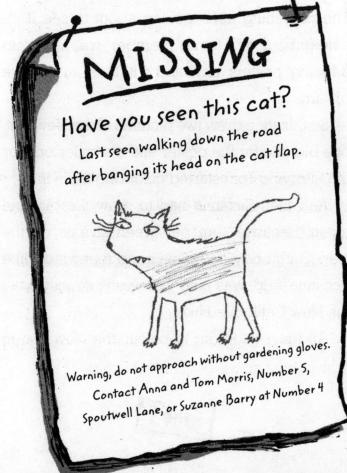

MISSING

Have you seen this cat?

Last seen walking down the road after banging its head on the cat flap.

Warning, do not approach without gardening gloves.
Contact Anna and Tom Morris, Number 5,
Spoutwell Lane, or Suzanne Barry at Number 4

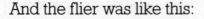

And the flier was like this:

MISSING If you have any information about this cat please bring it to the shed out the back of Spoutwell Lane, behind number 5 and knock three times and ask for Anna, or Tom, or Suzanne

And then we all went to see how much money we had for the reward.

Suzanne asked her Dad for her pocket money, which is meant to be three pounds fifty, but after Suzanne's fines for not eating her onions, and for losing her shoes, and not coming home straight from school, it was only eighty five pence.

I had already had my pocket money, and next week's. I asked Mum if I could have the week after next's as well, but she said, 'No, you can't. You do this every week. When it's spent it's spent.' I checked in my pocket to see if I had any left. There was only £1.49.

Tom said he had lots of money. Which he always does. Because he doesn't have anything to spend it on so it just adds up. He brought his moneybox out to the shed, and we opened it up. And tipped the money out on the table. And I counted it. And Suzanne said she didn't think I had counted it right. So I said, 'You count it then.' And she did. Out loud, and when she was finished, she did it again, to check. And she took ages. And said every sum out loud. And I undid my trainers and did them back up again, because

I was sick of hearing sums. Because I don't like them in school, and I especially don't like doing them on a Saturday, in the shed, when it isn't time for maths because it's supposed to be time for finding out who took the New Cat.

Suzanne put the amount for the reward on the bottom of the poster, and the flier, which was £26.79. And then we started to make more. Suzanne drew another outline of the New Cat, a big one for the poster and small for the flier, and Tom started colouring them in, and I had to keep an eye on him so he didn't do it green stripes with red feet again. And I wrote the words. And put the reward amount on the bottom of each one. It was already starting to get dark, and we had only finished two posters. 'If we had a photocopier we could make as many as we liked,' I said. There's a photocopier in Suzanne's house.

Suzanne said, 'No, we're not using it.' Because last time, when we tried to photocopy her Dad's dictionary, because he wouldn't let us borrow it, Suzanne's Dad went mad about us using all the paper. And the ink. And because the photocopier overheated. And he said, **'THE DICTIONARY IS TWENTY ONE THOUSAND THREE HUNDRED AND FORTY THREE PAGES LONG, FOR CRYING OUT LOUD, SUZANNE!'** And he had to get a man to come out and fix it.

'There's a photocopier in the cottage at the church,' Tom said. Which was true. And it was Sunday the next day.

So Suzanne said that in the morning we should all get up early, and go to Sunday School, to use it. And afterwards we could put loads of posters up, and hand fliers out, all around the village.

And then we heard Suzanne's Dad in the back lane, saying, **'SUZANNE, YOU'RE LATE. I WANT FIFTY PENCE OF THAT POCKET MONEY BACK!'** And Suzanne took it out of the reward money on the table. And changed the amount on the poster and the flier. And then she went home.

CHAPTER 12
Cats

I set my alarm and, in the morning, when it went off, I went into Tom's room and woke him up. Tom got out of bed and put his Spiderman suit on, with the built-in muscles. I wasn't sure if you're allowed to wear a Spiderman suit in Church. But Tom said he would put his coat on top, and wear his smart shoes, and leave the mask behind. So I said it was alright. Because once Tom has decided what he's wearing, it's hard to make him change his mind. Unless you pin him down. Like Dad had to, for a wedding, when Tom was meant to be a page-boy

and he refused to take his frog
wellies off.

Me and Tom had our cereal,
and brushed our teeth. And when we were ready
we went in to see Mum, who was still in bed.

Mum said, 'Why are you up?'

'For Sunday School,' I said.

Mum said she wasn't going to Church because
it wasn't her turn for handing out the hymn books
and she'd gone off it since everything with the
Vicar and his Koi Carp.

I asked if me and Tom could go on our own,
since we were ready.
Mum looked at the clock
and said, 'You're going to
be very early.'

So I said we would probably just sit and read

the bible, with Mrs Constantine, until everyone arrived.

Mum looked at me a bit strange, with her eyebrows up, like she does sometimes. And she shook her head, and said, 'Fine.' And she asked Tom, 'Are you going dressed as Spiderman?'

Tom said how he wasn't because he was going to put his coat on top, and his smart shoes, and he was leaving his mask behind.

And me and Tom said goodbye, and went out to the shed, and got the poster and the flier. And then we went next door to call on Suzanne.

We rang three times, and Suzanne's Dad opened the window really fast, and leaned out in his dressing gown, and shouted, **'YES? IS THERE A FIRE? IT'S SUNDAY MORNING, FOR CRYING OUT LOUD!'**

🐾 🐾 🐾

Mrs Constantine said it was nice to see Suzanne at Sunday School, because she doesn't normally come. And she asked what Suzanne would like to do.

And Suzanne said that she would like to use the photocopier.

And Mrs Constantine said, 'Oh.'

And Suzanne showed Mrs Constantine the 'Missing' poster and the flier about the New Cat.

Mrs Constantine said that the photocopier was only supposed to be used for things that were to do with the church, like the parish magazine, and hymn sheets, and community things.

Suzanne said, 'The New Cat was in the community. Before it went missing.'

And then Graham Roberts came in, and he said that he had seen the Vicar use the photocopier to copy a magazine, called *Pond Construction and Koi Carp Keeping*. And that wasn't to do with the Church. And then he said that he could show us how to use the photocopier, if we liked,

 because he had used it before, to photocopy his dog, before it died. And he brought a piece of paper out of his pocket, which was all crumpled, that had the photocopied dog on it. And he showed it to Mrs Constantine.

You couldn't see much, apart from the pads on the dog's paws. And a bit of fur. Mrs Constantine said, 'Alright, fine, but don't use all the paper. And if anyone needs the toilet today, you'll just have to whistle, because we're still without a door until the caretaker can put it back on.'

So me and Tom and Suzanne and Graham Roberts went upstairs to the room where the photocopier is, where all the old hymn books are, and the cloths for the altar, and the gold crosses. And Graham switched the photocopier on. And Suzanne gave him the poster, and the flier.

And Graham looked at them, and then he said, 'Emma Hendry has lost her cat as well. That's why she was upset at school on Friday. And that's why Mrs Peters said I should say sorry, even though I hadn't done anything, except paint her hair by mistake.'

Suzanne said, 'Joe-down-the road's babysitter Brian has lost his cat too.' And she said, 'So that's three cats that have vanished.'

And Graham said, 'There could be more.'

And Suzanne said, 'Yes.' Because, she said,

'Those are only the ones we know about.'

And Graham said, 'It's probably a *conspiracy*.' And he started the machine. And then he said, 'Have you ever heard of the Cat Lady?'

And Tom said he had, because he said, 'She's in *Batman*, and Batman is one of my best, after Spiderman, and Bob the Builder.'

Graham Roberts said, 'That's *Cat Woman*. She has cat ears, and a tail, and black boots. This is The *Cat Lady*. She doesn't look like that. She wears a blanket, and when it's raining she puts a carrier bag on her head, and she never has any shoes on.'

Tom said how he hadn't heard of the Cat Lady in that case. And neither had me or Suzanne.

Real
Unicorn
↓

Graham said, 'It's probably her who is kidnapping the cats.' And he said he would show us where her house was, if we liked, after Church.

Suzanne said she wasn't sure, because we would be busy handing out fliers, and putting posters up and all that. And because, like she told Tom afterwards, Graham sometimes tells lies, like the time it was Emma Hendry's turn to talk about 'Something I Like', on the carpet, in Mrs Peter's class, and she did it all about unicorns. Afterwards Graham told Emma that his Gran had a unicorn, on her farm, and Emma could come for tea, and see it, if she liked. And, after she went, Emma said that Graham's Gran's unicorn was only an old Shetland pony, that had an ice cream cone tied on its head, on a piece of elastic.

Fake
Unicorn
↓

119

Graham said, 'The Cat Lady's house is only in the market place. You can see it from the Church gate.'

So we said we would go. And the photocopier was finished, so we took the posters and fliers, and went back downstairs.

Mrs Constantine said it was time for the prayer.

Tom asked if she would put the New Cat in it. And Mrs Constantine said she would.

And then she said, 'Right, eyes closed, hands together.'

And she did the prayer, which went,

Dear God most high, hear and bless
Thy beasts and singing birds:
And guard with tenderness
Small things that have no words.

And then she said, 'And please take care of the New Cat, which is missing.'

And Graham Roberts said, 'It's been kidnapped by the Cat Lady.'

And Mrs Constantine said, 'Right...'

And Graham Roberts said, 'You can ask my Gran, because she knows all about her and she doesn't tell lies.'

And Mrs Constantine said, 'Amen.' Which means, 'So be it' and 'That's the end', and also, like Tom says, 'It's time for biscuits.' And Tom ate about ten. Until Mrs Constantine took the tin off him. And then we all went into Church for the last bit at the end. And the Vicar was saying, 'Ye have heard that it hath been said, an eye for an eye, and a tooth for a tooth: But I say unto you, that ye resist not evil: but whosoever shall smite thee on thy right cheek, turn to him the other also.'

And Suzanne whispered, 'See, Anna, *revenge.*'

🐾 🐾 🐾

When Church was finished, the Vicar went and stood outside, by the door. And when all the people came out, he shook their hands, and asked if he would be seeing them at Evensong, and told them to 'Go in peace and serve the Lord.'

And then me and Tom and Suzanne gave each person a flier, and said, 'And look out for the New Cat.'

When everyone was gone, Graham Roberts said, 'Follow me' and we went over to the Church gate. And we looked through it. And Graham pointed to a big house, on the other side of the market place, and he said, '*That* is where the Cat Lady lives.'

And then he went home.

Me and Tom and Suzanne stood and looked at the house. Suzanne said, 'It doesn't look like anyone lives in it.' Which it didn't. Because all the paint on the front was cracking, and peeling off. And two of the windows were broken, and one had cardboard in, instead of glass. And there were lots of tiles missing from the roof. And there was a bird's nest at the top of the drainpipe. And the chimney looked like it might fall off. And there were dead plants in the window-boxes.

We crossed the market place to look at it close up. Next to the door was a big window, like you get in a shop. The window was so dirty you could hardly see through it.

I wiped it with my sleeve but it didn't make much difference because most of the dirt was on the inside. Behind the window, a little way back, was an old net curtain, which had gone all greasy and grey. And, in front of the curtain, on the window ledge, there were three fruit boxes, like you get from the greengrocers. And inside each box was a dirty old blanket. And on top of each blanket, was a cat. Beside the cats there was a sign. I breathed on the window and wiped it again, and tried to read what the sign said. 'These... cats... are not... forced to sit... here. They do so of their own... free... will...'

Me and Tom and Suzanne looked at each other. And then we looked back at the sign.

Suzanne said, 'If nobody lives here, who wrote the sign?'

And Tom said, 'And who looks after the cats?'

And I said, 'Maybe Graham Roberts is right about the Cat Lady. And the Kidnapping. And the Conspiracy.'

We pressed our faces against the window.

'Let's put the posters up and go home,' I said.

But we stayed, looking. Then the curtain twitched, and I saw two hands, pulling it apart, and in the gap, above them, there was a face, with a blanket round it, and it looked out, and its eyes were wide, and its mouth was open.

I screamed. And the face in the window screamed back.

And I dropped all the posters and fliers.

And Suzanne said, **'RUN!'** And we did.

And we didn't stop until we got to the shed.

CHAPTER 13
The Stakeout

We locked the shed door. And stood against it. And we stayed very quiet.

After ages, Suzanne popped out the little knot of wood in the spy hole. And looked through.

Tom was jumping from foot to foot, like he does when he gets excited. And then, if he doesn't get to the toilet quick, he wets himself and gets upset.

'Do you need a wee?' I said. Tom nodded his head. He reached for the door. 'Don't open it,' I said. 'Can't you go in the shed?' I looked around for something.

'No!' said Suzanne, 'he can't.' And she got the

binoculars down from the shelf and opened the door a crack, and looked up and down the road. 'Quick. Just go there, on Miss Matheson's side.'

Tom's not really allowed to wee outside because, last time he did it, when Mum saw him, from in the kitchen, she tapped on the window, and said, '*Oi*, do you *mind*? Those are my herbs. We don't want your pee in our shepherd's pie.' But he didn't look like he would make it into the house. So I held the shed door open, and kept watch, just in case the person whose face we saw in the window had followed us.

Once Tom was back inside, and I'd locked the door again, Suzanne started writing on a piece of paper:

Whose was the face in the window?
Was it the Cat Lady?
Has she got the New Cat?

And she said, 'These are the things that we need to find out.'

'How?' I asked.

And Suzanne said, 'We'll have to go back to the house. Who's going to come?'

I said, 'Urm...'

Tom said. 'I am.'

So I said I would too. 'But only to look, from far away, like in the Churchyard, through the gate, or from behind the stone cross in the market place, through the binoculars.'

Suzanne said, 'It will be a Stakeout.' And she wrote, Anna's and Suzanne's And Tom's Plan to stakeout the Cat Lady's House on the top of a piece of paper. Only she wrote it 'steak out.' And she said how detectives do 'steak outs' all the time.

I looked 'steak out' up in my dictionary, which

wasn't easy. And, when I found it, this is what it said:

> **stakeout** [steyk-owt] ✦ *noun*
> the surveillance of a location by the police, as in anticipation of a crime or the arrival of a wanted person.

And then we looked in Suzanne's dictionary as well. And it said:

> **stakeout** [steyk-owt] ✦ *noun informal*
> a period of secret surveillance of a building or an area by police in order to observe someone's activities

And Suzanne said that after we had done the stakeout, we would probably have to do a raid, which is where you shout, **'GO GO GO'**,

129

and bash down the door, and stomp up the stairs, and shout, **'HANDS IN THE AIR'** and **'YOU'RE SURROUNDED'** and all that.

And then we made list of things to take with us.

Anna's and Suzanne's And Tom's
Plan to ~~Steak out~~ Stakeout
the Cat Lady's House

Things We Will Need

1. Coffee and doughnuts (because that's what Suzanne said that the police always have in stakeouts)
2. Binoculars
3. Sunglasses (for a disguise)
4. Watch (so we know how long we've been looking for)
5. Notepad and pen

6. Gardening gloves and Cat Carrier in case we find the New Cat

<u>What We Will Do:</u>

1. Watch the house

I said, 'What about a newspaper, with eye-holes cut out, for looking through?'

But Suzanne said, 'You don't have those in a *real* stakeout, Anna, that's just in cartoons actually.'

I hate it when Suzanne says 'actually', so I said, 'Well, some things that happen in cartoons happen in real life as well, actually.'

And Suzanne said, 'Like what?'

And I couldn't think of anything so I said, 'Lots.' And then I said, 'It's not like you know everything about stakeouts.'

And Suzanne said she did, actually.

And I said I didn't think so, because she didn't even know how to spell it.

131

And that's why she had put an 'e' in the middle, which is a piece of meat, like you eat for your tea.

Suzanne said how you didn't have to be able to spell things to know how to do them. And I said that you did. And Suzanne said, 'Then how come I can do a triple side somersault?'

And I said, 'You can't. Because I've seen you try and it's just like three wrong way round forward rolls.'

And Suzanne said it wasn't three wrong way round forward rolls and she wasn't going to do the plan for finding out about the New Cat or anything until I admitted that she could do a triple somersault, and that she knew all about stakeouts. And I didn't say anything. And after ages, I said, 'Sorry.' But only very quiet, and fast, and with my fingers crossed behind my back.

🐾 CHAPTER 14 🐾
The Cat Lady's House

Me and Tom and Suzanne stood behind the stone cross in the middle of the market place, and peered round, and watched the house through the binoculars.

'Oh, *look*!' Suzanne said. And she passed them to me.

Part of the window had been cleaned, and one of the Missing Pet posters which I had dropped, with the picture of the New Cat, had been put in the place where the dirt was wiped away. The sign about the cats not being forced to sit there was still on the window ledge. And the cats were there as well.

And not just three of them, one in each box; this time there were six. And one got up and stretched, and looked out of the window, and scratched itself. And then it jumped down behind the curtain, so we couldn't see it any more. And then another cat came up, from under the curtain, and pushed its way into one of the boxes, and fell asleep.

'How many cats are there?' Tom said.

And Suzanne said, 'We'd better keep track.' And she got the notepad out and wrote a number, for each cat, down the side of the page, and wrote what each one looked like beside it, like this:

cat number	looks like
1	Ginger, fat
2	black with bits of white
3	Siamese, skinny
4	tortoiseshell, bits out of its ears, one funny eye

We kept count of the cats like that as they came and went from behind the curtain. Tom was the best at spotting them.

And it was me who said if they had any marks, that made them stand out, so we would know know it again, like, 'black paws', or 'a piece missing out of its left ear' or 'three legs'. And Suzanne added them onto the list.

And, after a bit, we took it in turns to eat our sandwiches, and drink our juice (which we had instead of the doughnuts and the coffee because

Mum said she didn't have any doughnuts, only Kit Kats and she wouldn't make us a flask of coffee, and she was starting to get suspicious). And I ate Tom's sandwich as well as mine, because he said he didn't want his, because he only wanted the biscuits.

And, after ages, it started to rain, and we had to keep wiping our sunglasses, and we still hadn't seen the New Cat, even though we had 23 others in the notepad.

And then Suzanne said, 'Let's stop the stakeout for today,' because it was getting too dark to see the cats, and if she wasn't back for her tea she would get in trouble off her Dad. So we started to pack up. And just when we were about to go, something grey shot up into the window, from behind the curtain, and pounced on the tail of the cat with three legs, which had been hanging down over the window ledge. And the three-legged cat fought back. And then all the cats went mad, and started attacking one another. And you couldn't tell what cat was which, you could just see fur and eyes and teeth and claws.

Tom said, 'That was *it*, Anna. That was the *New Cat*.'

Tom wanted to go and knock on the door and ask if he could take the New Cat home.

But Suzanne said that wasn't what you did in stakeouts, because then the person being staked would know what was going on, and then Tom would have Blown Our Cover.

Tom said, 'Oh.' And then, 'I think I'll go anyway.' Because you can't really stop Tom once he has decided to do something.

And he came out from behind the cross, and ran over the road, and knocked on the door. Just like that. No one answered. So he rang the bell. But no one came.

Suzanne looked through the binoculars. And then Tom walked round the side of the house. And started opening the gate. So me and Suzanne came out from the stakeout spot, and ran after him.

When we got there, Tom was already in the back garden.

'It's a bit messy,' he said. Which it was. There was an old mattress, and a sofa, and a frying pan. And lots of things that don't normally go in the garden. And there were more cats as well.

Tom knocked on the back door. We heard a noise, from behind it.

'Someone's coming,' Suzanne said.

'Quick,' I said, '*Run!*' and I started to go.

But Suzanne and Tom didn't follow and, when I looked back, there was just a big ginger cat, coming out of the cat flap.

Tom said, 'I'm about the same size as that cat. Maybe I could get through the cat flap', and he put his head through it. And then he tried to get his shoulders in. But they wouldn't fit. So he took off his coat and tried again. And then he took off his Spiderman suit with the built-in muscles in.

And me and Suzanne got The Hysterics, watching Tom trying to get in, because he looked pretty funny just in his shoes and his pants.

And then we stopped having The Hysterics because Tom was gone. And we hadn't really thought he could actually get inside. Because Tom has tried to get in the cat flap at home, lots of times, and he always gets stuck. We looked in through the back windows, but they were too dirty to see, and there were all sorts of things piled up behind them.

We banged on the back door, and ran round the front, and rang on the bell, and I shouted, 'TOM!'

And then Suzanne started saying how it was her tea-time, again, and how she would get in trouble off her Dad if she was late and all that.

And I said, 'We can't leave.' Because what if Tom was tied up, or trapped, or dead? And because I was supposed to be looking after him, and we were only supposed to be in the shed.

And then I saw Tom's head coming out through the cat flap. And he wriggled his shoulders through. And he said, 'She's too busy looking for something now. And then she has to go shopping. We have to come back for the New Cat another time.'

And Suzanne said, 'Who?'

And Tom said, 'The Cat Lady.'

Suzanne looked at her watch. 'Let's go,' She said.

And there wasn't time for Tom to put his Spiderman suit on, so he just did

141

the first popper up, on his coat, and he didn't put his arms in, so it looked like a cape. And we ran home. Our fastest.

When me and Tom got in, we could hear Suzanne's Dad through the wall. Shouting about the time, and Suzanne's tea, and how it was cold.

Mum wanted to know where me and Tom had been, and why Tom only had his coat on.

'In the shed,' I said.

But Mum said she had checked. And then she asked Tom. And Tom said how we had been to the Cat Lady's house, and done a stakeout and Blown Our Cover and all that. And how we had seen the New Cat. And how he got in through the cat flap. And Mum wasn't pleased. Because she said how she had told us already about poking about in other people's property, and we were not to do it. And under no circumstances should we go in through other people's cat flaps.

Tom said, 'But what about the New Cat?'

Mum said that after tea she would go and knock on the door herself, and ask if the lady had the New Cat, and if she did, she would bring it back.

Me and Tom were waiting on the stairs when Mum got back.

'Did you get the New Cat?' Tom said.

'No,' said Mum. 'Nobody answered.' And then she said, 'I don't want you going down to that house again. It doesn't look safe.' And then she said how we had to come home straight from school every night, and we weren't to go out of the road on our own again unless she said. Mum said she would call at the house again, later in the week, and maybe someone would be home then and she would ask about the New Cat then.

🐾 🐾 🐾

When everyone was in bed, Suzanne knocked three times on the wall. And I knocked three times back, and we climbed up into the loft, and across the beams, to the hole in the wall, and we talked about everything up there, like the New Cat and the Cat Lady. And how Mum said she was going to try to get the New Cat back. And how, if she didn't, we could say we were going to Sunday School again next week, and go back ourselves.

CHAPTER 15

The New Cat's New Home

Mum went down to the Cat Lady's house three times but she never came back with the New Cat.

And the Cat Lady had told Tom we had to come back another time. So when Sunday came round, we told Mum we were going to Sunday School. Which was nearly true because Sunday School was very nearby. And if we got the New Cat back, like Suzanne said, we could go to Sunday School afterwards.

We went round the back of the Cat Lady's house and Tom squeezed in through the cat flap again. And he opened the back door. And me and Suzanne went inside.

It was dark in the Cat Lady's house. And it

didn't smell very nice, a bit like the Real Smelling Cesspit, at the Viking Centre where we went on the school trip. It was even messier inside the house than it was in the garden. There were boxes, and books, and hats, and papers, and picture frames in piles against all the walls. And there was a bald mannequin, and a broken coat stand,

and a stuffed deer's head, and some dead flowers, in the sink.

Suzanne said, 'Is this the kitchen, do you think?'

I said I wasn't sure because it was hard to tell, because if there was an oven, or a washing machine, or a fridge, they must have been hidden under piles of things. It was like the Brownie jumble sale, before Brown Owl has sorted everything into stalls for clothes, and bric-a-brac, and white elephant and all that, when all the bin bags have been emptied into the middle of the floor. Only it was more like a hundred Brownie jumble sales. Because some of the piles went right up to the ceiling.

We heard some rustling, and a crashing sound coming from the next-door room.

'That's her,' Tom said. And he opened the door, and looked through, 'Hello?'

'Send them away, Polly,' a voice said. 'I'm not inclined to receive this Sunday.'

And then there was more rustling and banging and crashing. And a saucepan with no handle came whizzing past, and then a shoe, and then a stuffed owl, which hit Suzanne on the head.

'Ow,' Suzanne said.

The Cat Lady came out from a pile of things, backwards, and she was coughing from the dust, and she turned round and saw us standing in the door. She looked frightened. 'What do you want?'

'Our cat,' said Tom.

'How did you get in here, did Polly let you in?'

'No,' said Tom. 'I came in though the cat flap.'

'Ah, in that case, I apologise. If it's small enough to get in by itself, it's small enough to stay, that's what I say. I had thought you were someone else.' And then she whispered, *'someone official.'* And she looked around her in case anyone was listening. 'I should have known by your height, I suppose, but they start them so young these days, and they're often undernourished. A policeman knocked lately and if it wasn't for his hat, I'd have sworn he was the paperboy.'

And then the Cat Lady put her hand to her forehead, 'I was looking for something, just now, and I can't remember what it is… Do excuse me a moment…'

And she went into another pile of things, and she rummaged around, and started throwing things out behind her from inside it. And one of them was a pile of our 'Missing' posters, about the New Cat.

Suzanne picked one of the posters up and said, 'This is the cat we're looking for.'

The Cat Lady stopped looking for a moment. 'You've lost something, have you? How frustrating. I was looking for something myself just now, only I've quite forgotten what it is.'

Suzanne held out the poster. The Cat Lady looked at the picture. 'Ah, it's not an affectionate animal, but a marvellous mouser.'

The fat ginger cat, that we had seen last time, coming out of the cat flap, started rubbing itself against the Cat Lady's legs. 'I don't encourage them – the cats – you understand. They just come. But, once they're here, it would be awfully rude

150

not to offer them something. Some of them have travelled.'

And then she tipped a big bag of dried cat food onto the floor and all the cats came round, and starting eating it. And the ginger cat ate the most. And he guarded his patch, and if the other cats came near, he went for them. And, in about a minute, the food was all gone. And the cats went back to their places.

'They're all in good health, though, as you can see.'

They didn't look in good health to *me*. They were the skinniest, scraggiest cats I'd ever seen. Apart from the fat ginger one.

The Cat Lady said, 'He's been with me from the beginning. He was a mouser, too, in his youth, but now, as you see, he's gone to fat. I've had to enlarge the cat flap. But I'm forgetting myself – do forgive me – it's been so long since we've had company. Will you take some tea?'

Suzanne said, 'Yes please.'

The Cat Lady pulled a little bell out of her pocket, and she rang it, and she looked up, like she was waiting for someone to come, and she shook her head, and said, 'She sleeps so late these days. And who can blame her, of course, a whole life spent in service. Well, if we're to make it ourselves, we shall almost certainly require a kettle. You can never find one when you need one, and when you don't of course, there's ten all at once...' And she started looking through the piles again.

She didn't find a kettle but she spotted the saucepan without the handle that had gone whizzing past Suzanne's head, and she said, 'Ah ha. Here we are.'

And she went outside and filled it from the outside tap by the back door. And she came back in, and lit a camping stove. And she boiled the water on that. And she said, 'If I'd known you were coming I'd have had Polly bring out the best china.' And she rang her little bell again. And she listened. And then she banged with a broom handle on the ceiling, but no one answered.

'Deaf as a post. I should replace her I suppose but she's *not quite right,* and who else would take her?'

She rooted around inside her pocket, and brought out two tea bags, and she dropped them into the saucepan. Then she picked up four empty yoghurt pots, and she tipped them upside down, and a few dead flies fell out, and she blew the dust off, and wiped them on her skirt.

'This set is quite serviceable. Came down to me on Mother's side, if I remember rightly.' And then she brought two stools over, and two boxes, from a heap behind the front door, and a crate, which she turned upside down for a table. And she poured the tea into the yoghurt pots. And we all sat down. And she said, 'After you,' to Suzanne, and Suzanne said, 'After you' to me.

I didn't really want it to be 'after me' because the tea didn't look very nice, and there wasn't any milk, and because mine still had half a dead fly in. But I drank a bit anyway. Which burnt a bit because the tea was very hot, and the yogurt pot was starting to melt.

154

Tom said, 'Have you got any biscuits?'

'Biscuits, biscuits, now where would she keep such a thing?'

She rang the little bell again, and shouted, 'Polly' up the stairs. And she starting throwing things out behind her, from in the piles again. Until she spotted something on the floor, in the corner, and said, 'Ah ha. The very thing.' Which it wasn't really, because it was a beer mat, but she gave it to Tom, and he bit it, and then he put it down.

And he said, 'Can we look for the New Cat now?'

And the Cat Lady said, 'Of course, of course, it is so frustrating when one loses something.' And she took three candles out of her pocket, and lit them, and gave us one each to hold. 'Mother never held with electricity, and as time passes, I find myself more and more in agreement. It's terribly unforgiving. I shan't come upstairs with you if you don't mind. I never do, these days. I do hope you find your cat. I was looking for something myself, just now, and I've quite forgotten what it is...' And she went rooting through a pile again.

We started going upstairs.

And the Cat Lady called after us, 'Do excuse the papers and so on, which aren't quite organised. My filing system is not what it was, and Polly has grown quite hopeless. Still, no one was ever hurt by a little untidiness.'

And it *was* untidy upstairs, too. Even more untidy than downstairs. And more untidy than mine and Tom's bedrooms were, the week that Mum went away when Dad was in charge. And more untidy than the shed, and the cupboard under the stairs. And the pile of Dad's broken things up in the loft.

Because you couldn't see the carpet, except for in little paths, through the piles, and it was so dirty that your feet stuck to it, and you couldn't tell what colour it was. And you had to be careful not to knock into anything because, once, when Tom did, a whole pile of things collapsed, and clouds of dust came up, and cats scattered, and boxes, and a long lamp, and a set of brass fire irons, came crashing down, and nearly hit Suzanne on the head. Some of the rooms were so full we couldn't even open the door to look inside.

We searched in all the rooms we could get into,

but we didn't see the New Cat. It was quite hard to see *anything* with the candles, and the mess, and all the curtains being closed. After a while we started back downstairs. Suzanne went first. And me and Tom followed and, as we got near the bottom, when Suzanne put her foot forward, to tread onto the last step, something pounced on it, in the dark, with all its claws out, and it dug them right in, and sank its teeth into her ankle.

And Suzanne screamed, 'Agh!' and kicked her leg in the air. And the thing flew off, and hit the wall.

'It's The New Cat!' Tom said.

Tom tried to pick the New Cat up, and its ears went flat, and its fur went big, and it scratched, like it always does.

So we went and got the

gardening gloves, and the cat carrier. And we got the New Cat into a corner, and we shooed it into the cat carrier. And we took it to show the Cat Lady.

'A cause for celebration,' she said. 'I suppose champagne would be too much, at this hour, and a Sunday after all. And heaven only knows where Polly might have put it. But will you take some more tea?'

I didn't want any more tea, and nor did Tom and Suzanne. 'No thanks,' we said.

The Cat Lady looked disappointed. 'Have you got any stories instead?' Tom said. 'Because we could celebrate with one of those.'

'I suppose you know the story of The Cat That Walked By Himself?'

Tom said, 'No.'

159

And the Cat Lady said, 'Shall we have that one, then?'

And Tom said, 'Yes.' And we sat down.

And the Cat Lady lit some more candles, and even the cats went quiet, and she said, 'EAR and attend and listen; for this befell and behappened and became and was, O my Best Beloved, when the Tame animals were wild. The Dog was wild, and the Horse was wild, and the Cow was wild, and the Sheep was wild, and the Pig was wild - as wild as wild could be - and they walked in the Wet Wild Woods by their wild lones.'

And after a while the Cat Lady stopped, and put her hand up to her forehead, and said, 'Oh, I've just remembered, I was looking for something, wasn't I, just now, and I've quite forgotten what it is... Do excuse me...'

And she went into one of the piles, and started looking through it.

And me and Tom and Suzanne went out the back door and went home, with the New Cat, with its ears flat, in the carry case.

● CHAPTER 16 ●
Shopping

We opened the front door, and let the New Cat out of the cat carrier, and shooed it inside, and Suzanne took the carry case and the gardening gloves and put them back in the shed.

When Mum saw the New Cat she said, 'Where on earth did you find it?'

'At Church,' I said, before Tom said anything. Because even though I told Tom about a million times that he shouldn't say anything to Mum about being in the Cat Lady's house, and all that, because we're banned, Tom isn't always very good at lying, because sometimes he forgets, and tells the truth by mistake.

The New Cat sat still in the corridor, and looked around. And then it ran into the kitchen, and straight out of the cat flap.

'Oh,' said Tom.

I said, 'Maybe it's gone hunting and it'll be back in a bit.'

But it wasn't. And it didn't come back all week.

So when Sunday came around, me and Tom told Mum we were going to Sunday School again, and we called on Suzanne, and we went back to the Cat Lady's house instead.

Tom went in through the cat flap, and let me and Suzanne in, just like last time, and we told the Cat Lady how the New Cat had gone missing.

And the Cat Lady pointed to the corner where the New Cat was after a mouse.

Suzanne tried to get the New Cat away from

the mouse, because it was still a bit alive, and the New Cat went mad, and shot up the curtains, and upset one of the piles, and sent all the cats scattering. And the other cats started attacking each other, and you could just see fur and eyes and teeth and claws. And the mouse got away, through a hole in the floor.

The Cat Lady tipped a bag of cat food into the middle of the floor, and the cats all came round, and started eating. Except the New Cat, which was staring at the hole, where the mouse had gone.

Me and Tom and Suzanne closed in on the New Cat, and got it into the cat carrier, and closed the door. And the New Cat watched the mouse hole through the mesh.

And we sat down on the crates, and Tom asked

the Cat Lady to tell us the next bit in the story.

And the Cat Lady lit some candles and told us some more about The Cat That Walked By Himself.

And after that we took the New Cat home again. And this time we pushed it in through the cat flap, like it had come back on its own. And then we went in ourselves and put the lock on. And we put some pieces of ham in the New Cat's dish and the cream off the top of the milk. And it had a nap, in its basket, with one eye open. And when it woke up, it tried to get out of the cat flap, but it couldn't because of the lock, so it just banged its head. And after that it went and waited by the front door, and as soon as someone opened it, which was Mum to let Pam in, the New Cat ran through it.

After that, Suzanne said that she didn't think there was much point in getting the New Cat into the cat carrier every week, and getting all bitten and scratched, and bringing it back. Not if it was only going to run away again. Which was probably true.

And Tom said that, next time, he didn't mind if we just visited the New Cat at the Cat Lady's house, and took the gardening gloves so he could stroke it, and listened to the rest of the Cat Lady's story.

The next Sunday, after Tom had stroked the New Cat, the Cat Lady asked, 'Does anyone fancy a spot of shopping?'

Tom said, 'Yes.' Because he loves going to the shops, even when it's just the butchers and the greengrocers and all that. Because he carries a bag, and sits up on the counter, and dips his wellies in the horse trough on the way past.

I don't like shopping, not like Tom, because normally it's pretty boring, unless it's for sweets. So I said, 'What will we be shopping for?'

'We can hardly know until we find it,' said the Cat Lady.

Which is different from going shopping with Mum because she always knows exactly what she's shopping for, because she has it on a list, on the side of the fridge, that says, 'milk' and 'bread' and 'braising steak'.

But the Cat Lady went past all the food shops, and she went in the charity shop instead.

167

She looked around, and picked things up, and asked the man, 'How much is this?' about things. Even though they all had the price on the bottom.

And the man told her, and then the Cat Lady said, 'Dear, oh dear, that's daylight robbery.' Even about a whole set of cutlery for 50 pence. And then she said, 'We shall go elsewhere.'

And after that we went into the park, and along by the river, and the Cat Lady said, 'Keep your eyes peeled.' And she poked in the bins, and then we saw a skip, and the Cat Lady got quite excited. And there were all sorts of things in there that somebody didn't want, like a broken toilet seat, and a tap with no knobs on, and a big rusty hinge.

And me and Suzanne found a few things we thought the Cat Lady would like. Like a bin to put her rubbish in, and some net curtains that looked brand new, and four china cups, which weren't even chipped. But the Cat Lady said, 'You take them. That's not the kind of thing I need.'

And then Tom found a bag of jam-jar lids, all different sizes, and a leg off a chair, and a pair of glasses, with the glass missing, which only had one arm. And he showed them to the Cat Lady.

And the Cat Lady said, 'Marvellous. Well, what a wonderful eye you have.' And she put them straight in her trolley. And when the trolley was full she said, 'That's enough for today.'

And we went back to the house.

Tom and the Cat Lady looked through the things that they had collected. And they found places to put them. And they were both pretty pleased. And the Cat Lady made us some tea, and Suzanne got the china cups out, which we had found. And I gave Tom the biscuit I brought from home. And we lit the candles, and sat down. Tom stroked the New Cat with the gardening gloves. And the Cat Lady carried on the story about The Cat That Walked By Himself.

'And the Cat walked by himself, and all places were alike to him. Of course the Man was wild too. He was dreadfully wild. He didn't even begin to be tame till he met the Woman, and she told him that she did not like living in his wild ways. She picked out a nice dry Cave, instead of a heap of wet leaves, to lie down in; and she strewed clean sand on the floor; and she lit a nice fire of wood at the back of the Cave; and she hung a dried wild-horse skin, tail-down, across the opening of the Cave; and she said, 'Wipe you feet, dear, when you come in, and now we'll keep house.'

CHAPTER 17

The Letters

After that we went to the Cat Lady's house every Sunday. And some days we got up early and went before school, too. And sometimes we said that we were staying behind after school for Homework Club, and went then as well.

You can do anything you want to at the Cat Lady's house. Me and Suzanne put a rope swing up in the garden. And we built a bonfire. And we found a carrier bag full of tins of sardines and cooked them outside on the camping stove.

Once, when we were there, the doorbell rang. The Cat Lady froze. 'Shh,' she said, 'it's them.'

Me and Suzanne got down on our knees, and looked over the window ledge, through the net curtains. There was a man and a woman, in suits. They rang the bell again. And they waited. And then the man put a letter through the letterbox. And they went away.

Suzanne went to the front door and felt around on the floor, under the pile of things in front of it. And she pulled out the letter and gave it to the Cat Lady.

'I can't imagine where poor Polly will find the time to deal with all this correspondence,' the Cat Lady said. 'She's not educated, of course, but Mother took care to see she knew her letters, and, even in ill-health, her handwriting is immaculate.'

She put the letter in a carrier bag with lots of others. And then she said, 'Are we shopping?'

And Tom said, 'Yes.'

But Suzanne said, 'I think me and Anna will wait here and help Polly.'

And the Cat Lady looked pleased. And me and Suzanne were pleased too because we didn't really like going down the river bank, and looking for bits of rubbish, and getting things out of skips and bins, not like Tom. Shopping with the Cat Lady was Tom's best thing.

When they had gone, Suzanne went and got the carrier bag full of letters. And she tipped them out, onto the floor, and she counted them all. There were forty-four. And none of them had ever been opened.

Suzanne said, 'Let's put them all in order.'

So we did, by the dates on the envelopes, which said when they had come.

And we laid them all out in a long line on the floor. And some of the letters were from three years ago.

'I wonder what they're about?' Suzanne said. And so did I.

'Maybe we should open one.'

'Just one,' said Suzanne.

So we did. This is what the first letter said:

Dear Mrs Neville,

We have received numerous complaints relating to the build-up of refuse in the garden to the rear of your property, including several dozen black bin-bags, a double mattress, two Chesterfield sofas, and a fridge/freezer. This is a formal request that these items be removed, and the garden cleared to a reasonable standard. Should you require help with the clearance, please contact us on the above number.

Yours sincerely

Mr A Grabham
Senior Environmental Health Officer

And then we opened another one, from the same person, also about the garden, saying it had got worse, and how more people had complained, and asking if the Cat Lady would like someone from the council to come to her house and help her.

And then, after a year, there was one that said:

Dear Mrs Neville,

An examination of the exterior of your property, and a partial examination of the interior (through the rear windows) has found that its condition threatens both your own health and that of other property occupiers in the immediate vicinity. In particular, we are concerned to find evidence of rats and mice in and around the property (despite the presence of at least twelve cats). We also observed rotting food items and large quantities of animal waste, both inside and outside your property, as well as generally unsanitary and unsafe conditions.

As stated in previous correspondence, failure to keep your property clean, and clear of accumulations of refuse, presents a risk to public health and, as such, if the current situation does not improve, the council will intervene. Please contact us to arrange for assistance in this matter.

And there were letters giving times and days when people from the council would be coming to talk to the Cat Lady. And others asking to make an appointment. And there were leaflets about 'Health and Wellbeing in your Home', and 'Caring and Support Services in your Community', with questionnaires for the Cat Lady to say whether they were 'very useful', or 'quite useful' or 'not very useful', 'not at all useful' or whether she was 'unsure'.

And me and Suzanne filled the questionnaires

in, to post back. And we ticked the 'unsure' box.
And then we were down to the last letter, which
was the one that had just arrived. It said:

Dear Mrs Neville,

We have attempted to work with you to improve
the repair and condition of your property. However
this approach has not resulted in improvements.
We therefore see no alternative but to carry out
works ourselves. We shall require access to the
property over several consecutive days, with as
many return visits as deemed necessary, in order
to clear it of refuse and restore it to a reasonable
standard for habitation. If we do not hear from
you with alternative dates, we shall arrive to
commence the clearance on Monday 24th October.

And that was in a week.

CHAPTER 18
A Reply

After the Cat Lady and Tom got back from shopping, and showed us their things, and we had all had some tea, and Tom stroked the New Cat with the gardening gloves on, and the Cat Lady had told us the next bit of The Cat Who Walked By Himself, me and Tom and Suzanne went home.

And Suzanne took the carrier bag full of letters from the council, because we didn't think the Cat Lady would notice. And, like she said, 'Somebody better reply.' Because a few of them said **'DELIVERED BY HAND'** in red letters on the front, and they looked pretty important.

And because we knew that the Cat Lady wouldn't like it if people from the council came to clear her house out, because she doesn't let anyone in, except for the cats, and me and Tom and Suzanne. And because she hates throwing things away, even more than Dad.

So me and Suzanne started writing back, and we put at the bottom, 'from Polly' even though we had never met her and, like Suzanne once whispered when the Cat Lady was trying to get Polly's attention by banging on the ceiling with the broom handle, 'I don't think Polly actually exists.' We wrote back whenever we could, in break and lunchtime at school, and in the back of our rough books when we were meant to be working out sums, and at night when we were supposed to be in bed, through the hole in the wall in the loft. And this is what some of the letters said:

Dear Mr Grabham,

Thank you for your letter about Mrs Neville's garden. She does not require help with it though thank you very much because it isn't actually rubbish because I think you'll find most of it is ~~air~~ heir looms that came down to her on her Mother's side (who was a hard lady but fair and taught me my immaculate handwriting despite my time of life).

Yours sincerely

Polly

Dear Mr Grabham,

I think it is quite rude to go round looking in people's windows, actually, Especially their rear ones. And that is probably why I keep Mrs Neville's windows so dirty. Her health is good and so is her cats'. If her neighbours are not well that is not really Mrs Neville's fault. I hope they get better soon. Have they tried putting their heads over a bowl of boiling water and having some Heinz chicken soup? I have not been quite right myself lately, so I have got a little bit behind with the cleaning. I am better now though and will start picking up the cat poos.

From Polly

Dear Mr Grabham,

By the time you get this I will have put new curtains up, moved the cat poos, put the dead rats in the bin, and put some flowers that aren't as dead in the window boxes. I hope that this means you do not need to come on the 24th October. If you do come, Mrs Neville will be out shopping, and I am sleeping late these days (who can blame me after my life in service?) so I'm afraid you won't be able to get in.

From Polly

And, after that, a new letter came. It said:

Dear Mrs Neville,

In light of recent correspondence from your
employee, Polly, we are arranging for a new
inspection of your property. We hope to find
the conditions of your property improved
significantly. If we do not find these to be
sufficient, the clearance of your property will
be rescheduled for the following week.

Yours sincerely,

Mr Grabham

After that, every time Tom and the Cat Lady
went out shopping, me and Suzanne did jobs at

the Cat Lady's house. We raked the rubbish
in the garden and put it into bags, and lit a
bonfire, and burned it, and collected all the
broken glass. We cleaned the front window,
and scrubbed the front step.

It was hard to make things look tidy because
there was so many piles of things, and as soon as
we put some in the bin or on the bonfire, Tom
and the Cat Lady came back with a trolley full of
new ones.

One time, when Tom and the Cat Lady were
out, and I was looking around the house for dead
mice and rats, for burying outside,
and Suzanne was picking all the
cat poos up, and putting them in
a carrier bag, for burning on the
bonfire, the doorbell rang.

Suzanne said, 'It might be Mr Grabham, the council man, come to do the inspection.' We looked out over the window ledge, through the new net curtain. It wasn't the council man, though, it was Mum.

'*Anna,* I know you're in there.'

Me and Suzanne stayed still and didn't say anything. And after a while we heard something out the back, and we went to look out through the cat flap.

Mum was coming up the back garden, past the broken television, and the mattress, and the rolls of chicken wire. And she saw the bonfire, with the rubbish, and the cat poo burning on it, and she saw me and Suzanne looking out through the cat flap.

And she said, '*Home*, now.'

186

I said, 'We have to wait for Tom. He's gone shopping.'

'Shopping?' Mum said. 'Is that what you call it? Tom is home already, Anna.'

And she didn't say anything else, all the way up.

Suzanne went into her house. And me and Mum went into ours.

Mum said, 'Sit down.' And she told me all about how Mrs Constantine had called round, and how Tom was with her, and how she had found him looking through the bins out the back of the Church with Mrs Neville.

And how she had asked Mrs Constantine where I was. And Mrs Constantine didn't know.

And how Mum asked, 'Wasn't she at Sunday School?'

And Mrs Constantine told her how me and Tom

hadn't been to Sunday School for weeks.

And then Mum started shouting, like she never normally does, almost as loud as Suzanne's Dad, and she said, 'YOU LIED, ANNA, AND YOU LET TOM GO OFF WITHOUT YOU, WITH A STRANGER, LOOKING IN BINS, AND YOU AND SUZANNE HAVE BEEN PICKING UP RATS AND CAT POO, AND BURNING THEM ON BONFIRES. IT'S A MIRACLE YOU DIDN'T GET TOXOPLASMOSIS, OR WEIL'S DISEASE, OR BURN YOURSELVES ALIVE.'

I tried to tell Mum how Tom wasn't with a stranger because he was with the Cat Lady and they had only gone shopping. And me and Suzanne were just trying to tidy up, and how we wouldn't have burned ourselves alive because we have done all about fires at Brownies, and Suzanne has got her Fire Safety Badge, and she knows how to escape from a smoke-filled room and everything actually, and Mum said, *'ANNA…'* like she always does. But louder. **'***ENOUGH!'*

And she said that I shouldn't say anything else. And I should go upstairs. And think about what I'd done.

This is what my dictionary says about toxoplasmosis and Weil's Disease:

toxoplasmosis [tok-soh-plaz-moh-sis]
✦ *noun (pathology)*
infection with the parasite *Toxoplasma gondii*, transmitted to humans by consumption of insufficiently cooked meat containing the parasite or by contact with contaminated cats or their faeces

Weil's [vahylz] ✦ *noun (medical)*
a type of leptospirosis in humans, an infectious disease characterised by fever and jaundice, that damages the liver and kidneys, often caused by bacteria in the urine of rats

CHAPTER 19
The Cat Lady

Me and Suzanne missed going to the Cat Lady's house. But not as much as Tom did, going shopping with the Cat Lady, and stroking the New Cat with the gardening gloves, and hearing about The Cat That Walked By Himself and all that.

After ages, when Mum stopped being cross, she said if me and Tom wanted, the Cat Lady could come to our house. And she would call round and invite her.

'The Cat Lady won't answer the door,' I said.

'I'll pop a note through,' said Mum.

'The Cat Lady doesn't open her post,' I said, 'because she thinks someone called Polly does it, who probably doesn't exist.'

But Mum went anyway, and she knocked on the door. And when no one answered, she put a note through, with our address on and all that, asking the Cat Lady to come. And she said, 'I'm sure she will if she wants to.'

But the Cat Lady never came.

After a while, me and Suzanne went back to doing things in the shed, and collecting worms, and making wasp traps, and all that. And Tom went up and down the road collecting gravel, and walking in a straight line with his eyes closed, and picking up litter with Mr Tucker.

And we didn't do much else because we weren't allowed past the bottom of the road by ourselves. Because Mum said we couldn't be trusted anymore.

Then, one day, which was Tuesday because Suzanne was there, when we were all having our tea, the cat flap flipped open, and the New Cat came in.

The New Cat looked wilder than ever. And its fur was even more matted, and one of its ears had a bit missing, and it was so skinny you could see the bones in its back.

Mum went and got some cat food and put it in the New Cat's dish, and the New Cat ate it all, really fast, and it kept looking behind it, like one of us might take it.

And after that it sat on the rug by the radiator. And Tom went and got the gardening gloves, and stroked it. And the New Cat didn't scratch, or try to get away. It just stayed still, and closed its eyes and fell asleep.

192

Tom said, 'The New Cat has probably come to see me, because I haven't been to visit, and soon it will go back.'

But the New Cat stayed all night. And, in the morning, it was still there.

On the way to school, we told Joe-down-the-road all about the New Cat and what had happened, and how it had come back. And Joe said that his babysitter Brian's cat had come back as well.

And at playtime Suzanne asked Emma Hendry if she had found her cat. And she said, 'It came back yesterday. All on its own.'

When we got home, me and Tom and Suzanne told Mum about how Emma's and Brian's cats had come back.

And Mum said, 'How strange, I wonder why.'

'We could go down to the Cat Lady's house and see,' I said.

And Tom said, 'If she doesn't answer the door, I can go in through the cat flap.'

And Mum started going on about how you shouldn't go poking round other people's houses, and going in through their cat flaps, and how the Cat Lady's house isn't safe, and all that.

And she said, 'I'll go and see if she's alright myself.'

When Mum came back she said, 'Nobody's home. There aren't any lights on. Maybe she's visiting relatives. I'll try again tomorrow.'

But the Cat Lady never has lights on. Because she doesn't like electricity. And, like Suzanne said, 'I don't think she's got any relatives.' And Mum going again tomorrow wouldn't make any difference because, like we already told her, the Cat Lady won't answer the door. Me and Tom and Suzanne went out to the shed and started trying to think of reasons why the cats had come back.

Tom said, 'I think the New Cat came back to see me.'

'I think it came back because it was hungry,' Suzanne said. Which was probably true. Because it was thin, and it had only been back for a night, and it had eaten four tins of cat food, three slices of ham, and two of Tom's biscuits, which it doesn't normally like.

Suzanne said, 'The Cat Lady must have stopped feeding the cats.'

'Why would she do that?' I asked.

'What if she ran out of cat food?' Tom said.

And Suzanne said, 'What if she just forgot?'

And I said, 'What if she's not very well?'

And Suzanne said, 'What if she's dead?'

Tom started chewing his sleeve.

'We need to go down and find out,' Suzanne said. But, like I told Suzanne, we couldn't do that because of being banned. And because of not being allowed past the bottom of the road on our own. And because ever since everything happened with the Cat Lady, Mum was always coming out and checking where we were, and what we were up to.

'There's no way we can go without Mum noticing,' I said.

But Suzanne said, 'There might be *one* way.' And she reached behind the stepladders, under the shelf with the wasp trap, and the worm box, and she pulled out the plan for going through all the lofts, which we did ages ago, before we started trying to find the New Cat.

The plan wasn't finished, because we had only written the title, which was 'Anna's And Suzanne's Plan To Find Out If There Are Holes In All The Walls In All The Lofts In All The Houses In The Road And, If There Are, Whether We Can Climb Through Them And Come Out In The House At The Bottom, Which is Joe-Down-The-Road's.' But Suzanne said we should try it anyway. Because she said we could just go up into my bedroom, and Mum wouldn't check on us if we were playing up there. And we could get up inside the loft, and go through all the holes, and come out at the bottom of the road, in Joe's. And then we could run down the village and check on the Cat Lady, and go back the same way, without Mum

197

knowing we had even left my bedroom.

'It's easy,' said Suzanne.

It didn't sound that easy, I didn't think, because for one thing we didn't even know if the lofts *did* all have holes in, or if they were all joined together. And for another thing when we got to the bottom, the hatch in Joe's house might be closed, and how would we get out?

Suzanne got a torch down from the shelf in the shed, and she turned it on, and she said, 'Who wants to come?'

And Tom said, 'Me.' And he put on his Bob the Builder hard hat with the torch on the front.

And we went up into my bedroom. And we

got up on the chest of drawers, and opened the hatch, and pulled ourselves up into the loft. And we got up onto the beam and balanced on it, and I told Tom how we had to step from one beam to the next. Which was a bit hard. Because Tom's legs are only little. And when we went across, he nearly missed the beam, and slipped, and he grabbed onto Dad's pile of 'useful' things, from the cupboard under the stairs, to stop himself falling off.

Dad's pile of things wobbled, and the toaster fell off the the top, and hit Suzanne on the head.

'Ow,' Suzanne said.

And then the whole pile collapsed. And all of Dad's things came down: the bag of worn-out footballs, and the broken tennis rackets, and the pile of newspapers he hasn't got round to reading yet. And the alarm clock that doesn't go off, and the kettle that me and Tom blew up by mistake. And the stool with one leg, and a bucket with a hole in the bottom, and half a broom handle without a head. And the boxes. And the bag of clothes from the olden days. And it went right through the ceiling.

'Oh,' Suzanne said. Me and Tom and Suzanne got down on

our hands and knees. And we looked through the hole in the ceiling, down to my bedroom underneath, where all Dad's things were on the floor.

And then Mum came running in, and she looked down at the pile of things on the floor, and she looked up at me and Tom and Suzanne through the hole, and she said, 'Are you three alright?'

And I said, 'Yes.'

And she said, '*Anna...*', like she always does, only a bit angrier, '*come down.*'

And we did. And Mum said how me and Tom and Suzanne had 'NO BUSINESS BEING IN THE LOFT.' And we were 'NEVER TO GO UP THERE AGAIN.' And she said, '*DO YOU HEAR ME?!*' And we did. Because she said it quite loud.

And Mum looked at the pile of things on the floor, and back up at the hole in the ceiling, and she said, '*PETE...*'

And Dad came in. And he saw the hole, and all his things, and how they had come through the ceiling. And he said, 'Ah, well, the thing *is*, you *see...*'

And Mum told me and Tom and Suzanne to go and play outside. So we did. And we could hear Mum talking to Dad from in the front garden. All about his 'rubbish,' and how she had been asking him to get rid of it for '*ten years*,' and how he was 'supposed to have taken it to *the tip*,' and how 'SOMEONE COULD HAVE BEEN *KILLED*.' And how now she would have to have a '*WHOLE NEW CEILING!*'

Mr Tucker was in the road, picking up litter.

'Hallo, Bods,' he said, 'sounds like the Blitz in there.'

We told him about how all Dad's things had fallen through the ceiling. And how Mum was cross. And what had happened with the Cat Lady, and the New Cat, and how it had come back. And how we wanted to go to her house, to check the Cat Lady was alright, in case she was sick, or dead, or she had run out of cat food or something like that. But we weren't allowed to go past the end of the road on our own.

'Not without a grown-up,' Tom said.

Mr Tucker said, 'A grown-up, is it, Basher? And, say you found one? What's the plan on landing, Popsie?'

I said there wasn't really a plan.

'Mmmmm,' said Mr Tucker. 'Take a dim view of that, very dim.'

'There *is*,' said Suzanne, 'but we haven't *written* it yet.'

'We just want to look,' Tom said.

'Quick shufti, is it? Recce, you say? Well, look here, bit hush hush, keep it under your hats but, technically speaking, I'm a grown-up myself.' Which was true. And Mr Tucker said he would come with us.

On the way we told him all about the council, and the letters, and how the Cat Lady doesn't answer the door, and how Tom goes in through the cat flap.

And Mr Tucker said, 'Cat flap? Not sure I like the sound of that.'

But me and Suzanne told Mr Tucker how Tom had done it millions of times. And how as soon as he gets in, he opens the back door, and lets us in as well.

And Mr Tucker said, 'Alright, aircrew, belt up: briefing. Basher, you're skipper; Old Lag's second Dicky. Popsie and Blondie, Arse End Charlies.' He looked at his watch. 'T.O.T. eighteen hundred hours. So, when I give the green, Skipper's off, in through the cat flap, back door open, bang on target, no silly beggars. Any offensive fire, straight out, Old Chap. All clear?'

And me and Tom and Suzanne said it was.

And Mr Tucker gave us the salute. And we gave him the salute back.

Suzanne opened the gate into the Cat Lady's back garden.

'Good God. Looks like it's been hit for a six. Righto, Old Chum, got your clobber?'

Tom took his coat off, and switched on the

torch on his Bob the Builder hard hat.

'Chocks away.'

Tom squeezed in through the cat flap.

Me and Suzanne and Mr Tucker waited.

After a while, Mr Tucker pushed open the cat flap. 'Alright in there, Basher?'

'I can't open the door,' Tom said. 'There's things in the way.'

And there were as well, because Mr Tucker shone his torch in.

There was more stuff than ever. And most of the piles had collapsed. And there wasn't enough room for Tom to turn round.

Mr Tucker said, 'Reverse gear, Basher. Backwards. Easy does it.'

But Tom didn't come back.

He wriggled a bit further forward.

And Mr Tucker said, 'That's far enough, Old Chum. Come back.'

And then we heard a crash.

And Mr Tucker said, 'Basher? Can you hear me, Old Chap?'

But Tom didn't answer.

And Mr Tucker shook the door handle, and then he leaned against the door, and pushed his shoulder against it. Then he walked down the garden. And when he got to the bottom, he shouted, 'Clear the runway…' And he ran at the door, and went straight into it with his shoulder. And the door burst open.

Tom was stuck under some boxes.

Mr Tucker pulled them off him.

'Look,' Tom said. And he pointed to the big

ginger cat, which was sitting at the edge of a heap of boxes and papers and things that had collapsed.

Mr Tucker shone his torch over. And he said, 'Good God.' Because, next to the cat, sticking out from under one of the piles of things that had collapsed, was a pair of feet, like happens when the house falls in the *Wizard of Oz*, only without the ruby slippers on.

Mr Tucker picked Tom up, and the big ginger cat. And he carried them both out, and then he took us all to the phone box, and he dialled 999. And said, 'Ambulance.'

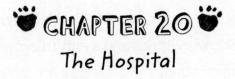
The next day, at school, everyone was talking about the Cat Lady. And how the ambulance had come. And how they had had to smash the front window to get inside. And move mountains of things before they could find her. And how they brought her out on a stretcher, with an oxygen mask on. And put her in the ambulance, with the lights on and the siren. And how it was Tom who had found her. And how Mr Tucker broke his arm, going in to get Tom. Which was all true. And that's why, after Mr Tucker took us home, Dad took him to the hospital.

After school, Mum took me and Tom and

209

Suzanne to visit Mr Tucker. Mr Tucker was sitting up in bed, with his arm in a sling. And Mum said, 'Thank you' again to Mr Tucker, for saving Tom.

And Mr Tucker said how it was Tom who was the hero, and how he 'ought to get a gong' and all that.

And Mum patted Tom on the head. And gave Mr Tucker some grapes and said, 'I'll be back for you all in an hour.'

Mr Tucker said, 'Right Wing: Debriefing.'

And we told him all about how the police put cones outside the Cat Lady's house, and tape that said, 'Keep Out.' And how there were three skips, and a fire engine, and two vans that said, 'Environmental Health', and people in white space suits bringing things out of the Cat Lady's house, in bags that said, 'Toxic.'

And Tom said, 'Do you think that the Cat Lady is alright?'

And Mr Tucker said, 'Ask her yourself, Basher.' And he pointed to the bed opposite. 'Not sure I hold with it. All this mixed ward business.' And he gave me the grapes and said, 'Take her these. There's only so many a man can eat.'

Both the Cat Lady's legs were in plaster, and they were up in the air. And she had lots of bruises from where all the things in the piles had fallen on top of her. And the nurse told us we should be quiet because the Cat Lady wasn't well, and she was a bit confused, and how they thought she had been trapped on the floor for three days.

The Cat Lady didn't recognise me and Suzanne. But she smiled at Tom. And she patted the bed, beside her, and Tom sat on it. And she stroked him on the head. And Tom gave her the grapes, and asked her to tell us the rest of the story, about The Cat That Walked By Himself, because we never got to the end.

And the Cat Lady said, 'Then the Man threw his two boots and his little stone axe at the Cat, and the Cat ran out of the Cave and the Dog chased him up a tree; and from that day to this, Best Beloved, three proper Men out of five will always throw things at a Cat whenever they meet him, and all proper Dogs will chase him up a tree. But the Cat keeps his side of the bargain too. He will kill mice and he will be kind to Babies when he is in the house, just as long as they do not pull his tail too hard. But when he has done that, and between times, and when the moon gets up and night comes, he is the Cat that walks by himself, and all places are alike to him. Then he goes out to the Wet Wild Woods or up the Wet Wild Trees or on the Wet Wild Roofs, waving his wild tail and walking by his wild lone.'

And Mr Tucker started snoring in the bed opposite.

And then the Cat Lady fell asleep as well.

And me and Suzanne ate the rest of the grapes, and Tom ate Mr Tucker's biscuits, until Mum came to collect us.

🐾 CHAPTER 21 🐾
Cleaning the Cat Lady's House

That's pretty much everything that happened with Tom, and the Cat Lady, and the Great Cat Conspiracy.

All week, people went in and out of her house while the Cat Lady was in hospital. And they cleared everything out, even the carpets, and the wallpaper, and after they cleaned it, and made it so you could tell what each room was, people came in to paint the walls, inside the house and out, and the window frames, and the front step, and the door. And they put new glass in the windows, and new tiles on the roof. And made the chimney so it didn't look like it was going to fall off. And people said it took twenty-six skips to take all the things away and make the Cat Lady's house tidy.

On the day the Cat Lady came back from hospital, Mum came with me and Tom and Suzanne to take her some flowers, and Mr Tucker came too, with his arm in a sling, and he brought the ginger cat, which Mrs Tucker had been looking after.

A nurse opened the door.

The Cat Lady was sitting in her front room, and she was looking at the wall. The nurse went into the kitchen to put the flowers in a vase.

And me and Tom and Suzanne and Mum and Mr Tucker all sat down. On chairs. Because all the boxes and crates had gone. The Cat Lady looked a bit scared. She was holding her hands tight

215

under her chin. She looked around the room. And she saw her little bell, on the mantelpiece, and she rang it. And she looked up at the ceiling. And, very quietly, she said, 'She's deaf as a post. One ought to replace her but who else would take her, at her time of life?'

And then the nurse came in, and she said, 'Can I help?'

The Cat Lady looked scared. 'How did you get in here? Did Polly let you in?'

Mr Tucker said to the nurse, 'Prob'ly do with a brew up, I think.'

And the nurse nodded her head and went to make some tea.

The Cat Lady looked worried. She put her hand on her forehead. 'I was looking for something, just now,' she said, 'and I can't remember what it is.'

She started looking around the room, and wringing her hands.

Tom opened the catch on the cat carrier. The ginger cat walked out, and it went over to the Cat Lady, and rubbed itself against the Cat Lady's legs, in the plaster casts. The Cat Lady picked the cat up, and closed her eyes, and held it tight.

🐾 🐾 🐾

Mum let me and Tom visit the Cat Lady after that. And for six weeks someone brought her meals on wheels and did all her cleaning, and looked after her while her legs were in plaster.

And then, when the Cat Lady got her casts off, the nurses and the helpers stopped coming. And the Cat Lady was pleased because she said, 'Polly does everything I need in the house. And

I'm quite capable of doing my own shopping.'

And sometimes when we went, Mr Tucker came with us, which the Cat Lady didn't like much, because she said, 'How did you get in? Did Polly let you in?'

And Mr Tucker said, 'Spot on, Squadron Leader. Sit tight, shan't stop, quick shufti.' And he picked up some rubbish from the corner and put it in his black bin bag.

And the Cat Lady said, 'She had no business inviting any old Tom, Dick or Harry in off the street,' and she whispered to her cat, 'The man is *quite mad.*'

Mr Tucker said, 'That's it, tiggerty-boo, I shall get weaving. Chocks-away.' And he gave the Cat Lady a salute. And the Cat Lady looked at the wall. And Mr Tucker went home.

Mr Tucker came quite often, and picked up the litter in the Cat Lady's garden, and tried to keep things tidy in the house. And so did me and Suzanne. Because, after the nurses and the helpers stopped coming, the Cat Lady started making a little pile of things at the bottom of the stairs, and leaving things in the sink, and once when we went, we couldn't see the kitchen table, and the time after that she had tipped cat food on the floor. And then, one day, we saw, behind the curtain, on the window-ledge, there were three fruit boxes, with blankets in, and there was a sign next to them that said, 'These cats are not forced to sit here. They do so of their own free will.' And, slowly, after that, the cats started coming again.

The End

Have you read the first two investigations?